THE HOT NURSE'S NYMPHO SISTER

IRENE TROON

The Hot Nurse's Nympho Sister

Past Venus Press
London 2009

Past Venus Press
is an imprint of
Erotic Review Books

ERB, 31 Sinclair Road,
LONDON W14 0NS
Tel: +44 (0) 207 371 1532
Email: enquiries@eroticprints.org
Web: www.eroticprints.org
© 2009 MacHo Ltd, London UK

Illustrations by Michael Faraday

ISBN : 978-1-904989-56-1

Printed and bound in Spain by Litografia Rosés. Barcelona

The Hot Nurse's
Nympho Sister

Irene Troon

THE HOT NURSE'S NYMPHO SISTER

The O'Brien Sisters. Annie O'Brien, a hospital nurse, is almost ready to choose her man and settle down to wedded bliss. But before she makes this final choice she feels she must indulge her lustful instincts in a string of raunchy encounters with both sexes.

By contrast, Jeanette, is already wed and trapped in an unhappy marriage. She is utterly dissatisfied with her husband's lacklustre lovemaking as well as her dull domestic life; to compensate she embarks on a voyage of unbridled affairs; through her sexual promiscuity she discovers her true sexuality as well as some revealing truths about her marriage.

Two sisters, two problems, two resolutions.

PART ONE

CHAPTER ONE

With her crisply starched white uniform pushed up around her waist and the cheeks of her ass perched on the edge of the desk, Nurse Annie O'Brien opened her thighs and exposed her cunt to Dale Rivers.

Dale was the pharmacist at the Clinton Peak Hospital. He was a soft-spoken guy, a bachelor in his early forties, and everyone who worked at the hospital liked him. He always flirted a little with Annie, in that mild way of his, and she never thought anything of it. Until this morning. Right after she started her shift, Dale approached her and announced he'd give both his arms and legs for the opportunity to go down on her.

That special feeling of a man's mouth on her pussy was something Annie always relished. It was never so completely satisfying as a good, hard cock in there, but it had a special meaning all its own. It proved to her beyond any doubt that the man craved to please her. And Annie liked to be pleased.

She told Dale it was unnecessary to give up his arms and legs. She told him he most likely needed them in order to work in the hospital pharmacy. She pulled him into an empty office and proceeded to unceremoniously reveal the object of his desire.

Since Annie never wore panties, the revelation was rather sudden. She'd always felt constrained and completely sexless in white pantyhose. A white garter belt and white nylons gave her more freedom and made her feel sexy. Moreover, dispensing with panties meant she could take advantage of any sudden opportunity.

Though more important still, perhaps, a hairy, panties-free pussy framed by a garter belt and stockings always seemed to drive men crazy, particularly the doctors, and driving men crazy was something Annie had long ago decided was one of the most life-enhancing things she knew how to do. Maybe almost as good as eating chocolate chip ice cream. Although the advantage of chocolate chip ice cream was that she'd be able to enjoy it at the age of ninety.

The expression on Dale's face was thrilling. She quivered at the rapture in his eyes as he gazed at her pussy. She had dark hair, even darker at her crotch, and there was plenty of it. Tucking up her uniform to keep it from getting stained, she pursed her lips in a kiss. She leaned back on her hands and drew up her legs, hooking the heels of her white shoes on the edge of the desk. She glanced down at the gaping, flushed pink gash of her cunt, and then looked at Dale and smiled.

"It won't bite, Dale. It's what you wanted, isn't it? All for you. Warm it up, honey. Come on, I have to get back to the ward."

He pulled over a chair. He sat down with his face no more than a foot away from her open pussy. She smiled at the way the very sight of her pudenda seemed to hypnotize him. She could see his nostrils twitching as he sniffed her. A man had once told her that she smelled great 'down there' – like peaches, warm in the sunshine... or was it nectarines?

"I don't have much time," she said. "Maybe you don't like it. This was your idea, you know. Don't you like my pussy, Dale?" She let a little note of complaint enter her voice and made a sulky pout with her generous lips.

But if Annie was pouting, Dale hadn't noticed. He spoke without moving his eyes from her crotch. "It's gorgeous," he said. "I knew you'd have a nice one, but this is really beautiful!"

Annie smiled to herself. She felt more relaxed now. She knew he was going to be good at it. A man had to like pussy in order to be any good at sucking it. She wasn't really due on the ward for nearly an hour. She had all the time in the world – more than enough time to have his mouth and tongue send her up onto cloud nine.

"Come on, lover," she said. "It's time."

Placing a hand on the inner side of each leg, he moved his mouth to her cunt.

She almost cried out as she felt his tongue begin lapping at her pussy like a child licking an ice cream cone. His delicate touch was unexpected. Most men dug in immediately, filling their mouths with cunt-meat. She was always thrilled at the way they growled and slurped and made sucking noises. The gynaecology residents were usually the noisiest. Maybe it had something to do with frustration. They spent all day looking at pussies without being able to really do anything to them, and when they finally had one available they simply lost control. Ferocious sucking was delightful, but a little too chaotic. Annie liked the action to be more deliberate.

Dale was very deliberate. He'd now widened the area of his lapping to the insides of her thighs. He was giving her a tongue-bath, completely wetting everything with his saliva, from the tops of her stockings to her navel. At intervals, he zeroed in his tongue on her cuntslit and began sliding it from top to bottom and bottom to top until she shuddered. After a few minutes of being washed over by Dale's agile wet tongue, Annie's fat pink clit was out stiff and quivering, just as her inner lips were turgid and swollen. Once her clit came out, Dale maliciously avoided it. Slipping his tongue lower down, he pushed it deep into her cunt-hole.

Annie stared down at the top of his head and groaned softly. She could feel his tongue in there. The sensation produced by his long, eel-like, muscular tongue was delicious. He moved his tongue in and out like a small cock. He had a clever way of rubbing his nose on her clit each time he pushed his tongue into her wet cunt-hole. Then he would waggle it from side to side. She was flooded, not just wet. Cunt-juice was oozing out of her in a torrent. Dale finally pulled back and looked up at her with a juice-coated, glistening face.

"How am I doing?" he said.

Annie nodded. "It's wonderful, Dale. But maybe you could pay more attention to my clit."

He smiled. "Trust me. I know all about clits," he said. "I'm an expert."

His hands were on her legs again, pushing them apart, once more lowering his mouth to her sex. This time he slurped. The delicate stage was finished. He moved his tongue-tip around with pressure behind it, probing all her crevices and folds. He spread her legs wider still with his hands, and then buried his tongue as deep as he could get it in the grip of her cunt-hole. He made a 'Mmmmmm', humming sound that vibrated his tongue and brought shivers to her spine.

She pulled his face deeper into her crotch. She could feel her cunt-juice trickling down onto her asshole and it drove her wild. She hooked her legs over his shoulders and began moving her hips up and down. He struggled at first; half suffocated, but then regained his composure and resumed vibrating his tongue. When he finally rolled his tongue-tip over her swollen clit, she lurched up at him with a grunt.

"Oh yes, Dale, suck it!" she groaned. "Suck my clit!"

She rolled her ass and pushed her crotch against his chin. Holding him firmly by the head, she stroked into his mouth, pumping against his tongue. She was fucking him now, rocking her cunt back and forth on his face to bring herself off. She rode steadily up to her climax, crooning and wailing as she massaged her clit over his lips and teeth and nose and chin. When the spasms finally hit her, she held his head firmly in her crotch and came, thighs clutching and juddering, on his face. She fell back on the desktop with a deep groan and covered her sopping wet cunt with her hand, with a faraway look in her eyes and a dreamy smile on her lips.

After the session with Dale Rivers, Annie walked into the surgical ward. Her uniform's skirt was a bit wrinkled, her cap very slightly awry and, compared with her normally pristine appearance, she must have looked very slightly dishevelled. She hoped it wasn't too noticeable, but she could have sworn that Head Nurse Connie Hudson had sniffed and given her a strange, searching look. After checking over the chart on the ward desk, Annie hurried off to the washroom to clean up for the second time since leaving Dale. Connie Hudson had a notorious sense of smell, and Annie wasn't taking any chances. Annie secluded herself in one of the half-dozen cubicles in the nurse's john. She pulled up her uniform and perched on the edge of the toilet seat. She dabbed and blotted her pussy. She smiled at the way she quickly juiced up again at the touch of her own hand and wondered, for the hundredth time, 'where did all that juice come from?'. Her labia hung out drooping and swollen, not yet recovered from Dale's sucking. This was just one of those days. Her period was due soon and she knew her cunt would be steaming day and night until it happened. Bending her head down to watch, she eased two fingers into the grip of her vaginal muscles and moaned softly at the sweet sensation.

Jesus, it was good!

She wiggled her fingers and jabbed them in and out. She watched every motion, savouring it all, smiling at the lewd beauty of her masturbation. It was always better when she could see it, when she could watch the sucking mouth of her meaty cunt grasping at her fingers.

Annie O'Brien had two serious suitors at the hospital, two members of the medical staff who'd hinted at marriage – a cardiology resident named Jake Herriot, and an intern named Grant Silvers. She was certain she'd eventually wind up marrying one of them, but she had, no idea which one she preferred. Sometimes she drove herself crazy trying to decide between them. She thought about them now. She imagined them watching her, begging her to let them shove their cock into the channel of her pussy. She imagined them pleading on their knees. She'd make them eat her before they fucked her. She'd make them suck her pussy as she sat on the toilet and pissed a yellow stream. Jake had once done that to her, the kinky devil. He was much better at sucking than Grant. But then, Grant had the bigger cock...

She had three fingers in her cunt-hole, now. She stretched her cunt-mouth with one hand and used the fingers of the other hand to massage her clit. She was moving along to an orgasm – and the sensation was marvellous! She loved watching her hips bucking her drooling cunt against her hands. It was almost as if she were watching someone else masturbating. She gasped at the pleasure of it, moaning as the orgasm washed over her body in a great wave. Probing and massaging her cunt in a frenzy, she tried to milk every last bit of pleasure from the come.

Not yet sated, hoping to bring herself off again, she continued playing with her cunt. Whenever she masturbated, the second orgasm was always easier to bring on than the first.

The door to the washroom suddenly opened. She heard two nurses come in. Giggling silently at her audacity, she continued fingering her cunt. She clamped her lips firmly together to prevent herself from crying out. Carefully massaging her throbbing clit, she used every ounce of willpower to hold herself still and silent while she brought herself off for the second time.

She attempted to dry her pussy again. She wiped the sticky, pungent cunt-juice off her fingers with toilet paper. She arranged her uniform and left the cubicle. The two nurses were busily pissing in their own cubicles. With a sigh of relief, Annie slipped out the door.

At the end of the corridor, as she turned the corner, she ran into Jake Herriot.

"Jesus!" he said. "You're like a guided missile! Where in hell are you rushing to, Annie?"

She laughed nervously. She apologized. After a quick glance down the corridor to make certain they were alone, she pressed against him and kissed his cheek.

"Find an empty bed," she said. "And please do it fast!"

Jake chuckled. "That bad, huh? I haven't seen you moaning for it like this in ages."

She playfully pinched his cock. "Shut up and find us a bed," she said. With a final fingering of his rising cock, she pranced off to the surgical ward. She knew Jake would come through with a bed – he always did! She hoped he wouldn't dawdle.

As it turned out, he moved faster than she'd expected. An hour later they were facing each other in an empty room on the sixth hoof. Jake had arranged things with the nurse in charge and Annie felt safe enough to really let loose. God, how she needed it!

Removing his white jacket, Jake undid his tie. Annie kicked off her shoes and came into his arms. Their mouths locked in a hot, searching kiss. He pulled her close to him with one hand pressed on her quivering ass. The prominent bulge of his cock-shaft dug into tile rise of her belly.

Annie felt as if she had a fire in her cunt. She wasn't sure she'd be able to hold out through the preliminaries. Jake liked to dally he liked a long build-up!

His cock bulging into her belly, he helped her peel off her uniform. He unhooked her bra and removed it, staring hungrily as her large, red-tipped tits came into view.

"The best tits on the staff," he said.

She cupped one of her full tits in her hand,

offering it to his open mouth. Closing his lips over her hard nipple, he began greedily sucking on it.

Sighing, her hand holding up her tit, she fed his mouth.

He finally released her saliva-coated tit and moved his lips to the other one. Annie reached down between their bodies and lowered his zipper. Probing inside his fly, she grabbed hold of his hard cock and brought it out into the open air.

Jake moaned into the flesh of her tit when she began to rhythmically stroke his cock. She felt a drop of pre-cum ooze from his cock-slit onto the palm of her hand. Using the ball of her thumb, she spread the sticky drop over the tight skin of his fat cock-head.

"I can't wait," she said. "Fuck me now!"

He pulled his mouth off her tit and chuckled. "Easy, honey," he said. "I want a taste of that sweet pussy of yours."

He crouched down with his face near her pussy. With a sigh of resignation, she moved her legs apart to give him access. Using the fingers of both hands, her knees wobbly, her pelvis thrust forward, she pulled her cunt-lips open and offered herself.

"Suck it!" she hissed.

An instant later, she felt his rough tongue lapping the length of her burning cunt-slit. He quickly found her clit and began sucking on the quivering bud. Using his head for support, she twirled her fingers in his hair. He had a good mouth. He worked her flesh over, feeding on her, massaging her clit with just the right mount of pressure. Clenching the cheeks of her ass together, she tilted her cunt up to his face.

She finally pulled away from him. "Damn you!"

she said. "Get your clothes off and fuck me!"

She stretched out on the bed, her eyes on his throbbing cock still protruding from the fly of his pants. He quickly removed his clothes and lay down beside her. She grabbed his cock, pulling at his hard prick-meat.

"Put it in me!" she screamed.

He positioned himself between her legs. Grabbing her calves, he spread them apart and opened her cunt-gash to his hungry gaze. She moved her hands to her tits and fondled them. He rubbed his cock-head between her dripping cunt-lips. Grasping her calves again, he pushed them up so that her knees pressed into her tits. He positioned his throbbing cock-head at the entrance to her cunt and pushed forward to sink the length of his cock into her slippery pussy-channel.

She moaned at the full, stretched feeling caused by his pulsing cock in her cunt. He was in her to the hilt. Her arms went up and she grabbed his shoulders.

"Fuck me now!" she hissed. "Fuck me hard!"

The clutching walls of her cunt grabbed his cock as he slowly pulled out. When he had no more than his fat cock-head still inside, he thrust in hard and hit bottom. A gasp of pleasure burst out of her throat. He began a steady rhythm, pistoning in and out of her cunt with long, slow strokes.

She dug her fingernails into his muscular shoulders as he continued lunging into her body. His rhythm picked up speed. The base of his cock continually brushed over her throbbing clit with each stroke.

She soon felt his cock expanding in the grip of her cunt-channel and she knew he'd be coming soon. She was ready now. She wanted his cum.

She wanted him ramming her cunthole as he shot his load. She loved taking the jism out of a man. She loved sucking his balls dry with her pussy!

His strokes suddenly increased in speed and became jerky and erratic. He vetted a deep groan, and a moment later she felt the first hot spurt of his cum and began writhing in the throes of her own orgasm.

He continued to piston in and out of cunt as the boiling load gushed from bloated head of his cock.

"Oh, God!" she moaned. Shivering, she wrapped her legs around his ass and closed her eyes. They churned and writhed snaking the bed creak and bounce beneath them. A tremor rocked him as he shot the last of his load into her frothing cunt.

What he finally pulled out and rolled over on his back, Annie turned on her side and kissed his cheek.

"That was lovely," she said.

He turned his head and looked at her. "Then let's make it permanently lovely."

She laughed. "Is that a proposal?"

"You know it is."

"Then the answer is no," she said. "At least – not yet. And now, can we please just get the hell out of here before someone finds us like this?"

CHAPTER TWO

The first time Annie saw John Hacker, she knew he'd be a troublesome patient. He had two television sets and two telephones in his room. He was a gravel-voiced, muscular man who looked like one of those people who made sure they got whatever they wanted. His eyes, like hot black coals, raked over her body in a way that made her shiver. She had the impression he could see right through her clothes right through her uniform to the bare black bush of her pussy!

The first day she was alone with him, he told her she had a nice ass.

The second day, he asked her if her tits were real.

On the third day, he suddenly flung the sheet aside, pulled up the front of his hospital gown to his bare belly, and gathered his cock and balls in his beefy hand.

"I need action," he said.

Annie turned up an eyebrow and tossed him a look of annoyance. "This isn't a cathouse, Mr. Hacker. It's a hospital. You want action for that thing, you wait until you get out of here."

Grabbing hold of her hand, he pulled it down on his limp cock. "Play with it," he said. "See if you can make it hard!"

The feel of his cock had its effect on her. He had a stubby, circumcised cock with a fat, purplish cock-head. His balls were enormous. Her fingers automatically began stroking him, pulling the soft skin of his cock-shaft back and forth with a gentle touch. Then she decided she might as well milk him, if only to keep him quiet. She increased both the pressure and tempo of her pumping fingers. His cock began to swell anti stiffen. She curled the fingers of her free hand under his ball-sac and jiggled his balls.

"You're a sweetie," he said. "Show me your cunt."

"Don't be silly, Mr. Hacker."

"You've, got a bare pussy under that uniform,

haven't you?"

She chuckled. She liked his cock. She liked the strength of it. She also liked the merry look in his eyes. "What makes you think I'm bare?" she said.

"I can tell," Hacker said. "It's a sixth sense. Show it to me!"

The temptation was too great. Pulling her fingers away from his cock, she walked over to the door and locked it. She returned to the side of the bed. Slowly unbuttoning her uniform, she slipped it off and draped it over a chair.

His eyes glittering, Hacker gazed at her black haired pussy. "That eating stuff," he said.

She smiled. "Then I hope you're hungry, Hacker, because here I come."

Climbing over him, she moved her legs apart and straddled his face. Using the fingers of both hands, she brushed the curly black hairs away from her moist pussy. Her clit was up. Pink flesh gleamed her fat, hair covered cunt-lips. She petted her cunt-lips with her fingertips, easing them open, prying them wide apart.

"Kiss it!" she hissed.

Looking down, she watched him stick out his tongue. His nostrils quivered as he sniffed the aroma of her cunt. When he began stroking his tongue between her cunt-lips, she sighed and eased her crotch down onto his face.

He began eating her cunt with a fierce determination, his sucking mouth grinding on her oozing pussy-flesh. He lapped deep into her cunt-hole. He massaged her cunt-lips with his nose. He breathed in deeply the smell of her cunt, saturating himself with her female scent. His strong hands slid over her ass, squeezing and jiggling her rubbery asscheeks.

Shuddering with pleasure at the aggressive probing of his tongue, Annie finally moved her cunt off his face and left the bed.

"You're good at that," she said.

Hacker grinned and watched her strip off her bra. When she reached for a garter clasp, he shook his head. "Leave them on," he said. "I like a little spice in my food."

Wearing nothing now except her white cap, a white garter belt, white stockings, and white shoes, Annie cupped her tits in her hands and asked Hacker about his wife.

"She's dead," he said. "You remind me of her. Big tits and a juicy cunt. She was a good woman!"

Annie was glad to hear he liked big tits. She wanted more of his cute mouth, but this time on her nipples. When she sat down beside him on the bed, his hands immediately moved to her tits. She leaned forward to hang a nipple into his open mouth. She smiled at the way he handled her tits, at the way his hands held them while he nursed. He was a big, burly man but at the moment, he looked like an infant, sucking on her hanging tits as if they were filled with milk. She crooned encouragement as he moved from one nipple to the other.

Her nipples glistened with his saliva when she finally pulled away, from his face. She patted his cheek.

"You're really, in no condition to do any hard work," she said. "Why don't you just lie back and let me take care of you."

"Take care of me how?" he growled.

Annie laughed. "If you promise to behave

yourself, I'll suck your cock."

Hacker grinned. "It's a deal," he said.

She raised up head of the bed to make it easier for him to watch. She ran her hands over his legs and thighs. A sheen of sweat covered his protruding belly, flattening the line of graying hairs that thickened as they neared his crotch. His cock was limp again, and hung to one side like a tired sausage.

His body jerked as she slid a hand under his balls and worked her fingers in the crack of his ass. He groaned when she pushed a fingertip into the tight ring of his asshole. Lifting up his cock with her free hand, she leaned forward and rubbed it against her tits.

Lowering her face, she ran her tongue over the skin of his belly, tickling his hairs and stimulating his flesh. She nipped him in places with her teeth. She blew her hot breath into the tangle of his crotch hair. She continued moving her fingertip in and out of the tight grip of his asshole.

He moaned between clenched teeth, and she felt the first surging of blood into his limp cock. She cupped his balls and massaged them. She nuzzled her nose into the thick hair around the base of his cock.

She ran her fingertips back and forth along the underside of his slowly rising cock-shaft. His cock-head was visibly swelling now, fattening out to the size of a small plum. She kept working her fingertip in and out of his loosening asshole. He was getting there, his cock-shaft thickening and lifting, his cockhead expanding. He was soon grunting like a bull, his hands moving to pull her head down toward his upright cock.

She extended her tongue and teased it up the

underside of his erect prick-shaft. She moved her mouth down again and licked around his cock-root. Opening her lips, she sucked in one of his quivering balls.

Hacker groaned. She sucked on his ball, playing her tongue over his wrinkled ball-sac, probing and slurping. He groaned again when she popped it out of her mouth and sucked in his other ball. By the time she moved her mouth up to his cock again, his ball-sac was coated with her saliva.

She had all of her finger wiggling in his ass, now. He squirmed and shifted on her hand, grunting at each thrust of her fingertip.

Cupping his balls, she slipped her mouth over the throbbing head of his cock and took him in until his cock-head jabbed at the back of her throat. She began bobbing her head up and down, fucking him with her suctioning mouth.

"Oh, yeah!" he groaned. "Blow me, you bitch! Suck my cock!"

His fat cock was completely bloated now, a hard slab of fuck-meat sliding smoothly in and out of her mouth. When the bulb of his cock began to throb, Annie knew he was only seconds away from a climax. Squeezing his balls, stepping, up the rhythm of her finger pistoning into his clenched asshole, she chewed and gulped on his thrusting cock-meat.

"Oh, shit!" he groaned. "I'm coming, baby! I'm coming!"

Her lips pulled violently at his flexing cockhead. A sudden spurt of hot jism geysered out of his cock-head into her mouth. A slippery coating of cum soon covered her teeth. His cock continued to throb and pump what seemed like a never-ending supply of jism into her sucking mouth. She swallowed continuously as his cock-cream eased down her throat. She kept sucking him, trying to drain his balls – to draw every ounce of his cum out through his cock!

He fell back onto the bed, his eyes closed, his chest heaving, his lungs pumping for air. Annie lifted her head and let his soft, slippery cock slide from her lips. She licked up the remnants of jism at the corners of her mouth. She packed her tits into her bra and slipped on her uniform. She pulled down Hacker's hospital gown, covered his legs with the sheet, and checked his pulse. Humming softly, she walked out of the room.

Later that afternoon, Head Nurse Hudson stopped Annie in the corridor.

"We're having trouble with that Hacker patient," Nurse Hudson said. "He screams at all the nurses. Insists you're the only one he wants in his room. I don't know what's going on, dearie, but I've got orders to see that Mr. Hacker gets treated like royalty. See if you can calm him down, will you?"

Annie gazed at Nurse Hudson's plump ass as the older woman turned and walked off. Annie had never liked Head Nurse Hudson. There was something strange about her. Annie had heard rumors that Nurse Hudson liked women. There was always some of that going on at the hospital, and as long as it didn't affect her, Annie paid no attention to it. If Head Nurse Hudson enjoyed sucking pussy more than sucking cock, Annie felt sorry for her. Annie had no doubts about her own preference.

She found Hacker sitting up in bed with a

telephone at each ear. He motioned her to close the door and sit down. Remembering Head Nurse Hudson's request, Annie shut the door and sat down on a chair near the window. She sat there waiting for Hacker to finish what looked like two very important telephone conversations. She smiled when she noticed him ogling her legs. She remembered the feel of his fat cock spouting cum into her mouth. Her pussy quivered and she moved her thighs apart. She pulled back her uniform until her thighs were completely exposed. Sliding a hand down to her crotch, she gave him a teasing smile and fingered her cunt lips. By the time he was off the phone, she had him panting and growling like a grizzly bear.

"You promised you'd behave yourself," she said. "All the nurses are complaining about you."

"The hell with that," he said. "Let's fuck. That cunt of yours is driving me crazy!"

Annie laughed. The rampant lust in his eyes fed her own excitement. She thought of his cock again, and any hesitation she had about yielding quickly vanished. Walking over to the door, she turned the lock. Anyone on the staff could open the door from the outside, but at least she'd have time to get off the bed.

Moments later, she was on the bed completely stripped. Hacker's medical problems were minor, and she decided there was no reason he couldn't fuck her any way he wanted. It would probably be good for him. His cock was hard and throbbing, and he was obviously strong enough!

She opened her legs for him. He knelt between her knees. Instead of immediately crawling forward to mount her, he lifted one of her legs and began to lick the smooth, warm flesh above her stocking top. He licked up and down, and then he moved to her other leg and did the same thing.

"Great legs," he said. "A good pair of legs always turns me on."

He rolled over. She looked back over her shoulder as he gazed at her compact white ass. He briskly brushed his hand back and forth across her asscheeks, enjoying the way they quivered.

"Great ass!" he said. "You've got the sweetest little ass I've seen in a longtime."

He leaned forward and kissed her neck. His nibbling lips moved down between her shoulder blades to the small of her back. Wrapping his hands around the firm cheeks of her ass, he kissed down into her ass-crack. He licked and sucked at her damp, quivering assflesh.

She held her breath, waiting to see how far he would go.

He pushed his hot wet tongue deeper into the sweaty cleft of her ass. Soon, he was pressing his face firmly between her asscheeks, his nose caught at the top of her asscrack, his tongue probing and tickling at her tingling little asshole.

"Oh, Jesus!" she moaned.

He rose up on his knees. Gripping her at the hips, he pulled her ass up. She moved her knees forward for support. He pushed her thighs farther apart and pressed against the small of her back. He now had her kneeling with her head and shoulders on the mattress and her ass in the air.

He looked directly down at her fat, dark haired cunt and winking asshole. Grabbing his cock, he worked the head of it into her juicy cunt. Ht pushed forward. She vented a grunt of approval as his thick cock sank smoothly into her slippery cunt.

Pumping, twisting, slamming his belly against her bouncing ass, he fucked her from the rear. She moaned, writhed, and pressed back against his thrusts. His cock-shift felt wonderful as it rammed in and out of her steaming cunt like a piston. At the end of each stroke, his balls slapped deliciously against her dripping cunt lips.

He suddenly pulled out of her. She rolled over on her back with a groan. Amazed, she watched him walk over to the sink and run cold water over his cock. He chuckled when he saw the look of surprise in her eyes.

"I'm cooling it off," he said. "I don't like my gun to go off until I'm good and ready." Then he added: "How'd you like to do something different?"

"Like what?" Annie said.

"You ever had it in the backdoor?"

Annie laughed. "It's been a while since the last time," she said. "But let's try it. We'll have to use something, though. What about your shaving cream?"

Hacker chuckled. "Good idea," he said. He brought over a can of shaving cream. Annie anointed his cock with white foam, spreading it over the entire length of his stiff, bloated cock, and then she lay back on the bed to dab some on her asshole, inserting her finger deep inside, as far as it would go.

His eyes glittering, Hacker looked down at her target. Small, brown, shiny and puckered, her asshole lay between the proudly swelling mounds of her ass like a tiny wrinkled bud. "It looks awfully small," he said. "Are you sure that's where you want it?"

Annie ignored the silly question. She climbed up on her hands and knees, lowered her head and shoulders to the mattress, and offered Hacker her ass.

"Go to it!" was all she said.

His cock twitching, Hacker bellied up to her asscheeks. He aimed his fat, rubbery cock-head at her asshole. Annie moaned when she felt his cock-head rubbing against her asshole.

"Come on, lover," she said. "Get it in!"

Holding his cock in place with one hand, he steadied himself by holding onto her hip with the other. He pushed forward. At first, her asshole refused to open up, but then Annie suddenly relaxed and his cock-head snapped into her tight ass-channel. He continued pushing forward, slowly sliding the length of his cock into her hot, rubbery ass-tunnel.

"Oh shit!" Annie groaned.

"Are you okay?"

"I'm fine!" Annie said. She loved having a cock in her ass. It always hurt a little, especially when the man had a thick cock, but after a moment or two her ass-muscles reined and the only thing left was an incredibly pleasurable feeling. She adored a cock in her pussy, but her ass was about ten times more sensitive. She reached a hand back and worked her fingers between her cunt-lips. If Hacker could last long enough, she'd be able to get an orgasm going in both her holes!

Taking hold of her hips, he began thrusting his cock. Each jab of his fuck-meat into her ass brought a cry of total pleasure from her throat. She kept her fingers working on her clit. When she pushed a finger into her cunt, she could feel his cock on the other side of the partition between her cunt-hole and asshole.

She suddenly heard a noise coming from the

direction of the door. She thought it was the door, but she wasn't sure. She thought the door had been opened and closed again. Maybe it was another nurse. Maybe someone had seen her on the bed with Hacker's cock up her ass! Oh, God!

But at this point, she didn't care. The cock up her ass was too delicious. "Fuck me!" she groaned. "Keep fucking me!"

CHAPTER THREE

When she finally arrived home that evening, the memory of the door opening and closing while she was on the bed with Hacker brought on a fit of depression. She'd been a damn fool for taking a chance like that with a patient. If someone had really opened the door and seen her – and it could only be someone on the staff! One word to the Director of the hospital would get her fired. Peter Sikorski was very strict about things like that. He didn't mind nurses screwing around with doctors – especially when he was one of the doctors – but the patients were out of bounds. Sikorski had more than once made a pass at her, but Annie had never accepted his invitation. She now realized the only way to protect her job was to make sure the Director would be on her side.

Knowing what she had to do, Annie decided it was best not to waste any time. She called Sikorski at home. He was a fifty-year-old bachelor, and she hoped he might be able to see her that very evening. The essential part of her plan was that she get to Sikorski first.

He seemed happy to talk to her on the phone. He seemed even happier when she came right out and invited herself to his house. A mischievous smile was on Annie's face when she hung up the phone. Poor old Sikorski would never know what hit him!

She decided to dress carefully. She wore a simple, carefully fitted short dress whose neckline revealed just the right amount of the tops of her tits. Under the dress, she wore a pair of flimsy bikini panties, a thin garter belt, and sheer beige stockings. The nylons came up very high – to just an inch below the mound of her pussy.

An hour after the telephone call, she was on Sikorski's doorstep.

"Come in, come in, Annie," he said. "You look marvellous. You're still the prettiest nurse in the hospital."

Annie fluttered her eyes and laughed coquettishly. "Oh, really, Dr. Sikorski!"

"Peter Sikorski never lies," he said. She walked with him into his large living room. Even at fifty, he was still extraordinarily handsome. He had a full head of steel-grey hair and icy blue eyes, and his high cheekbones betrayed his Slavic origins. He made her sit down on a low sofa. He brought her a drink and sat down opposite her in an easy chair. Dressed as she was, there was no way she could sit gracefully on the sofa without showing a good deal of her thighs. Her knees were nearly up at her chin, and the slightest displacement of her short dress would reveal the tops of her stockings, the bare undersides of her thighs – and even the bulge of her cunt-lips under the thin nylon of her panties! She gave him just the briefest glimpse of what she had on under her dress, and she smiled inwardly at the resulting sparkle in his eyes.

"I think it's important that as Director I be close to everyone on the staff," he said.

Annie nodded. He was wearing a silk dressing gown, and she rather wondered if he had anything on under it. The more she studied him, the more attractive he became. Getting the suave and elegant Director on her side was not going to be as unpleasant as she'd thought!

His eyes were now on the neckline of her dress. He ran his tongue over his thin lips. She imagined that tongue vibrating up and down between her cunt-lips. The idea of Sikorski sucking her pussy made her shiver with lust. She had to be careful, however. If she moved too fast, Sikorski might get suspicious.

As if unconscious of what she was doing, she flashed the undersides of her thighs at him again. From the gleam in his eyes, she guessed he'd probably seen the bulge of her nylon covered cunt-lips. There might even be a damp spot there – she could feel some of the wetness now!

When he shifted his body in the easy chair, she couldn't believe her eyes. The movement of his legs had opened the front of his dressing gown. He pushed himself forward on the seat until his cock and balls hung over the edge in full view. His cock dangled over a wrinkled, leathery ball-sac. He was uncircumcised. His fat cock-head was out of proportion to the thin stalk which it capped. His cock-head, still half covered by foreskin, was almost as big as a plum.

He smiled at her with a twinkle in his eyes. "I know why you're here," he said.

Annie's mouth fell open. "Huh?"

"Head Nurse Hudson told me all about your little party with one of our patients."

"Party?"

Sikorski sighed. "The patient's name is John Hacker. Hudson says you had his cock up your ass."

"Oh, God!" Annie moaned. "Does that mean I'm fired?"

"That depends on you, my dear."

"On me?"

His cock-head was visibly swelling, his prick-shaft twitching as it slowly lengthened.

"You know the rules about activities of that kind with patients," Sikorski said. "Hudson and I agree we ought to have a good reason to ignore something like this. So far I don't see any good reason."

"What would be a good reason?" Annie said.

Her heart was beating like a trip-hammer. It was up to her to change Sikorski's mind about firing her. The sight of his dangling cock made her shudder. His cockhead was throbbing and his prick-shaft was growing.

"Open your knees," Sikorski said. "Let's have a look at your legs."

She looked up to see his eyes staring down at her legs. She slowly parted her knees. She spread her legs farther and farther apart, and then she took hold of the hem other dress and rolled it back to her belly.

"Lovely," Sikorski said.

She looked down at her slim legs, at her swelling thighs clasped by her stockings. She ran her fingertips up over her thighs to the waistband of her panties. She began rolling down the flimsy panties covering the dark bush of her cunt-hair. When the panties were just a thin roll on her thighs, she ran the flat of her hand across her springy pubic curls. Sikorski's eyes were fixed on her crotch, concentrating on her moving hand.

"I just love Clinton Peak Hospital," she whimpered. "I'd be awfully depressed if I had to leave."

His cock was rigid and ready for fucking. His swollen cock-head looked almost as big as a baseball on the end of his thin cock-shaft. He had the fattest cock-head Annie had ever seen!

"You've got a lot of hair there, haven't you?" he said, his voice tinged with something bordering on awe. She smiled inwardly. Sikorski was obviously a 'bushman'.

She slipped off the sofa and knelt on the rug. Picking up the hem of her dress, she peeled her dress off in one smooth motion and tore it away. Rising to her feet, she rolled her panties down to her ankles and stepped out of them. She readjusted her garters. She stood naked in her thin garter belt and beige stockings; her feet perched on high-heeled pumps, wide apart.

"Come over here," he said. He was breathing heavily. His hands reached out to her. When she moved forward, his hands came around behind her to grip the cheeks of her ass. He opened his legs wide and pulled her in. With a low grunt, he pressed his face forward and buried his nose into her bush of cunt-hair.

Annie felt Sikorski's agile tongue probe between the fat, wrinkled lips of her cunt. He moved his hands to the front to pull open her outer pussy-lips and give him better access to her core. She stood motionless as he sucked and licked at her cunt. Then he pulled his mouth away and turned her body around.

"Let's have a look from the back," he said.

Her pussy quivered as he forced her to bend over. Moving her legs apart, she doubled over and took hold of her knees with her hands. If he wanted to look at her that way, she would make sure he saw it all!

Sikorski gasped. "Christ, what a delicious-looking cunt!" he said.

A soft moan escaped her lips at the first touch of his wet tongue on her nut-brown asshole. He played his tongue-tip over the slightly raised ring of her asshole. The sensation made her clench tight and she automatically squeezed her ass muscles. The feelings produced by his tongue as it repeatedly circled her asshole was exquisite. Electricity seemed to spark from his tongue-tip to her very core in a way that was almost unbearably pleasurable.

At intervals, he ran his tongue lower down to probe the mouth of her cunt. She could feel the first stirrings of an impending orgasm. Her nipples were stiff. Her tits hung down like heavy fruit, swaying each time she moved her body. His desire to impale herself on it, spear her ass on his wet tongue. His tongue-tip finally squirmed into the grip of her asshole and her throat gurgled out a moan of pleasure.

He tongue-fucked her, making powerful little stabs at her asshole, for a full two minutes. Unable to take any more, Annie pulled away and turned to face him. Her nipples were stiff and swollen. Cunt-juice dripped down the insides of her thighs to wet the tops of her stockings. Looking down, she saw Sikorski had his cock in his hand. Pre-cum continuously leaked from the slit at the end of his cock-head.

She knew what he wanted. She knew what he

needed so badly – and she could give it to him. She kneeled down on the rug between his legs. She leaned forward with her hands on the chair on either side of his body. Extending her tongue, she began licking the end of his hard cock.

Her pussy fluttered as she worked on his half-bared cock-head. She opened her mouth and took the exposed end of his cock-head between her lips. The heat arid velvety texture of his cock-head was delicious. She loved the feel of his soft foreskin against her tongue.

Denting was soon grunting with pleasure. Annie gently tightened her teeth on his foreskin and slid her mouth down the shaft of his cock. She shivered at the feeling of his huge cock in her mouth, at the velvet-soft feel of his cock skin under her lips, sliding against the bone-hard flesh beneath. She began sucking on his bulbous, mouth-filling cock-head.

She had him now. Peter Sikorski might be the Director of the hospital, but at the moment he was completely in her power. Her head bobbing slowly up and down on his cock, she fucked him with her mouth. Sikorski groaned and bucked his crotch against her face. She worked his cock deeper into her throat, burying almost all of its length in her warm mouth – until he grabbed her head with his hands and pulled his cock from her mouth.

"Get your cunt over my face," he said.

She changed position, straddling his chest with her ass and cunt toward his face. He pulled her down until her crotch was against his mouth. Once again she engulfed his throbbing cock. She rammed her cunt as hard as she could against his face. Using his hands to hold her cunt open, he squirmed and wriggled his tongue up and down along its length.

She rocked her body back and forth, her mouth sliding up and down on his cock, her cunt moving up and down on his face.

He suddenly groaned, and a moment later spurted a great gob of jism to flood her mouth and clog her throat. His cock spurted again, and she gulped and swallowed to keep pace with his eruption. She kept her head still, except to caress the fat knob of his cock with her tongue. As his climax ended, the spurting of his cum dwindled to a mere convulsive twitching of his cock-head. She sucked gently on his cock in order to drain the last of his sperm. As the last drop rolled over her tongue, her cunt spasmed on Sikorski's mouth. She came on his face, her cunt-juice oozing thickly onto his nose and lips. She finally fell off to the side and lay on her belly.

"Delicious," Sikorski said. "Absolutely delicious!"

She felt his hand fluttering up the backs of her thighs. He cupped and fondled the cheeks of her ass. She turned her head to look at his body. He lay on his side facing her. His limp cock hung down across his thigh. Her head was still toward his feet. Her pussy quivered as he continued to stroke her asscheeks.

Moving her face to his crotch, she took his soft cock between her lips. She curled her fingers under his balls. She tongued back his foreskin to expose his meaty cock-head. She swirled her tongue over his velvety skin, her fingers gently stroking his soft cock-shaft.

Sikorski continued caressing her asscheeks. When she opened her legs to give him, access to her cunt, she felt his cock-head swell in her mouth. His fingers probed between her cuntlips as his cock continued growing. Lying on her belly, she still held no more than the end of his cock in her mouth. She shivered at the tickling touches of his fingers along the lips of her pussy. She moaned when his fingertips briefly brushed her asshole. He rubbed one cunt-lip against the other, teasing the hairs that covered their surfaces. Her cunt-hole opened like a hungry mouth to the probing touch of his fingers.

His cock was now fully erect again, and she removed her fingers from his cock shaft. She began to suck his cock-head, her lips forming a tight ring behind his flared cock-rim. She used her lips and tongue, and occasionally she nipped the resilient flesh of his cock-head with her teeth.

He now had two fingers in the channel of her cunt. She shuddered as he slowly pistoned them in and out of her juicy pussy-hole. His cock-head, swelled in her wet mouth. She closed her right hand around the shaft of his cock, pulling back on it to completely peel the foreskin off his throbbing cock-head. She closed her mouth over his fruit-like cock-head, her tongue massaging the knot of flesh on the underside. The ring of her tightly closed lips prevented his foreskin from covering his cockhead. She now had almost four inches of his cock in her mouth! The slit of his cock-head was leaking pre-cum, teasing her with a hint of the jism she wanted spurting in her mouth. She wanted to taste this cum again, to drink him until his balls were drained. She kept tonguing and sucking him with a steady rhythm.

His fingers were brushing her asshole, again. She shivered when she remembered the feel of his wet tongue. She loved being touched there. Only a few hours had passed since John Hacker's cock had stretched her asshole, but her little ass craved attention again. She mewled and wriggled her hips to encourage Sikorski. Instead of reaming out her ass with a finger, which was what she hoped for, he forced her off his body and pulled his cock out of her mouth.

Taking hold of her hands, he helped her to her feet. He led her to the end of the sofa. He stood behind her, his cock pressing against her ass.

"Bend over," he said. "Hold onto the sofa!"

She let herself be pushed forward, her hands outstretched to hold the arm of the sofa, her feet planted wide apart on the floor. She bent forward at the waist and heard him grunt behind her.

"Look at that," he groaned. "Christ, what an ass! Look at the way your tits hang down. I'm going to fuck your brains out, my dear!"

He pushed her shoulders down until she had her cheek against the sofa. He clutched her hip with one hand and used the other hand to guide the spongy head of his cock into the mouth of her dripping cunt.

"Oh, shit, yes!" she moaned. Her pussy grabbed at his cock, welcoming his stiff prickmeat.

Gripping the cheeks of her ass with both hands, he spread her open to feed the length of his cock into her juice-drenched cunt. Her hands caught at the sofa when he lurched forward and buried his cock to the hilt. He pulled back with a deep grunt of satisfaction. She could feel her cunt-lips pulled out by his cockhead as he withdrew. Then he pushed forward again, his cock sliding home with a long, twisting stroke.

"I think you ought to be in my office the first thing every morning," he said. "Ten or fifteen minutes of this in the morning will get the day off to a good start, don't you think?"

"Mmmmmmmm!" she murmured.

He responded by quickening his strokes thrusting, his cock solidly into her cunt, faster and faster, until she and the sofa shook from the force of his driving cock. She was beginning to feel the first sensations of an oncoming climax. She moaned at the slippery, frothy feeling of his hard cock stroking in and out of her steaming cunt. Her swollen cunt throbbed with each powerful thrust.

"Fuck me!" she moaned.

The swinging of her upraised ass became more pronounced. She gyrated her cunt in order to feel all of his meaty cock reaming out her cunt-channel.

"Give it to me!" she cried. "Fuck me hard!"

Panting and wheezing, his hands trembling on the white checks of her lewdly tilted ass, he pumped his cock vigorously in and out of her boiling cunt. At the end of each stroke, his balls slapped against her upper thighs with a wet noise. Grinding and humping, she dug her fingernails into the upholstery of the sofa. She shook her ass, pulling and rotating on his thick cock.

"Uhh!" he groaned. "Uhh – oh, baby – I'm coming, coming!"

She came with him, her cunt vibrating, her ass humping, as his jism splattered into the clasping channel of her vagina.

Later, as they lay resting on the sofa, he told her Head Nurse Hudson expected a visit from her.

"Hudson isn't too bad," Sikorski said. "The best thing to do is relax and enjoy it!"

CHAPTER FOUR

Annie was thankful she was off duty the next day. Late in the morning, she opened her eyes, totally exhausted after a restless sleep. There was no escaping the fact that she had to see Head Nurse Hudson as soon as possible. She knew that if she waited too long, Hudson would only be more difficult to handle.

Sliding out of bed, rubbing her eyes as she crossed the bedroom to the bathroom, Annie prepared a bubble bath and climbed into the tub with a sigh. She wondered what her married sister would say if she knew she was preparing herself for a lesbian encounter with her head nurse, in order to save her job. Jeanette's sex life seemed so… simple and straightforward compared with hers. She imagined someone else's – a woman's – hands moving over her belly, her fingers curling in the wet hair at her crotch.

The hand between her thighs gripped her cunt. God, it felt good! Her cunt was already swollen from the heat of the water. She massaged it with her fingers, strumming it with a familiar cadence. The gash of her cunt seemed on fire. She pushed a finger into the grip of her cunt hole. She spread her legs wider. She rubbed her outer and inner cunt-lips with the heel of her palm.

Her leg muscles began to tremble. Her feet moved back and forth along the bottom of the tub. She totally surrendered her body to the delicious pleasure of finger-fucking herself!

She stared down at her vivid pink, quivering clit protruding from the black bush of her cunt-hair.

"Fuck!" she moaned. "Suck my clit!"

A gurgling sound came out of her throat. Her

hand closed over her cunt, her fingers pulling and pinching her cunt-lips – churning the creamy, thick juice oozing out of her hairy pussy-hole. The orgasm was better than nothing – but what she really needed was a cock, a big long cock plowing in and out of her cunt and dumping a load of hot male cum!

Climbing out of the tub, she dried her body with a large towel and began her preparations for Head Nurse Hudson.

An hour later, Annie was standing outside Nurse Hudson's office at the hospital. Annie paused a moment in front of the door. She fluffed her hair and straightened the neckline of her dress. Taking a deep breath, her heart pounding, she rapped on the door.

"Come in!"

Opening the door, Annie stepped into the office. Nurse Hudson was seated behind her desk. When she saw Annie, she raised an eyebrow and smiled.

"Close the door and sit down," she said.

There was only one empty chair in the room, and that was on Nurse Hudson's side of the desk. Feeling as if an invisible hand was twisting her stomach, Annie moved forward and sat down.

Nurse Hudson appraised her from head to foot. "I rarely get a chance to see you out of uniform," the older woman said. "You're very attractive."

Annie blushed. "Thank you," she said.

"You've already seen Doctor Sikorski, haven't you?"

Annie nodded. "Yesterday evening."

"Then I suppose we understand each other, don't we? You ought to consider yourself very lucky. I think any one of the other nurses wouldn't have a chance – they'd be fired immediately. But you're something special, aren't you Annie? Twitching your little ass around her like a bitch-dog in heat. I can smell it, you know. I can smell your precious little pussy every time it's been active. I had a hunch you'd get after that Hacker fellow. Pretty picture you made, up on the bed like that with your cute little ass in the air. Very pretty. He had you in the ass, didn't he?"

Frightened by the venom in the woman's voice, Annie nodded.

Nurse Hudson smiled. "And now, in a manner of speaking, you belong to me, don't you?"

Annie nodded again. She realized her hands were trembling, and she folded them over her knees.

Nurse Hudson fixed her eyes on the low-cut neckline of Annie's summer dress. "Stand up," she said.

Annie rose uncertainly to her feet. Her eyes gloating, Nurse Hudson leaned forward and ran her fingers over Annie's nylon-clad knees. A moment later, the woman's soft warm hands were moving up under Annie's dress and over her thighs. Annie froze. She'd expected Nurse Hudson's hands on her body, but now that it was happening, she was confused. She'd never experienced the touch of another girl's hands. Once in a while a girl would try to get familiar with her – brush her tits, pat her ass, or even try to rub cunts. Annie always discouraged them. This time, however, she had no choice. There was also something different about it. Nurse Hudson was at least ten years older than Annie – she was certainly not another girl. The axe was hanging over Annie's head. One wrong word, one unthinking act and she'd be canned – and her chances of getting a job at another hospital in town would probably be zero!

Annie stood there with her hands at her sides and her eyes straight ahead. She was afraid to breathe, let alone speak or move. Under her dress, Nurse Hudson's hands were on Annie's ass now, squeezing, clutching, and fondling her plump ass-cheeks covered by flimsy nylon panties.

Nurse Hudson pressed her face against Annie's belly. Annie found herself trembling with excitement. The touch of Nurse Hudson's hands somehow seemed more erotic than she'd expected! Annie wondered if the older woman could tell she was getting turned on.

Nurse Hudson finally sat back in her chair. She looked Annie up and down and smiled. "Take off the dress, honey," she said. "Let's have a look at you."

Her eyes glazed, Annie unzipped her dress and slipped it off. Nurse Hudson looked her over and nodded her approval.

"You're lovely." Nurse Hudson said. She waved a hand when she saw Annie had stopped undressing. "But take everything off," she said. "Let me see all of it, darling!"

Irritated now, confused by the dampness between her legs, Annie stripped everything off as quickly as possible. She'd be damned if she'd give Nurse Hudson the pleasure of a striptease. Nurse Hudson didn't seem to mind. By the time Annie was completely naked, the older woman's eyes were glowing.

"Delicious!" Nurse Hudson said. "Come closer, honey. Don't be afraid!"

When Annie moved forward, Nurse Hudson

extended her hands and took bold of Annie's heavy, swaying tits. Annie a shivered at the first touch of Nurse Hudson's fingers brushing lightly over her nipples.

"Mmmmmn, you excite easily, don't you?" Nurse Hudson said. She pulled Annie's tits towards her face. Annie moaned softly when the older woman began licking and sucking at her long dark nipples. She could feel her pussy quivering. She could feel her cunt-juice oozing out between her swollen cunt-lips to drench the insides of her thighs. She was turned on! There was no way to deny it!

The fact that Nurse Hudson was a woman didn't seem to make any difference – her nipples and cunt and clit didn't seem to care. One thing was certain – Nurse Hudson was an expert at sucking a tit. Hot flashes of exquisite pleasure radiated out from Annie's saliva coated tits. She looked down, to watch how Nurse Hudson drew the nipple and its surrounding dark flesh deeply into her mouth. Annie yielded to the delightful sensation of having her nipple sucked so expertly by Nurse Hudson. She knew, as she looked at her other tit and saw her nipple standing up hard, that the one in Nurse Hudson's mouth must also be erect.

Annie's heart was pounding in her chest. She was confused. She'd always thought two women playing with each other was the dirtiest thing imaginable! But the spreading feelings of pleasure that the expert tongue and mouth of Nurse Hudson were bringing to her entire body was almost more than she could bear!

As Nurse Hudson's hands roamed down Annie's sides, clutching at her asscheeks, the fingers digging into her yielding flesh, Annie instinctively moved her body forward against the older woman.

Nurse Hudson pulled her mouth off Annie's tit. The long, hard nipple glistened with saliva.

"Get up on the desk," Nurse Hudson said.

Annie knew what was coming. She perched on the desk, her ass on the edge, and leaned back on her elbows. Nurse Hudson was obviously going to eat her cunt. Annie found herself excited by the idea. Head Nurse Hudson had been giving her orders ever since she'd been working at the hospital. Now she was going to have her cunt-juice all over Head Nurse Hudson's face.

Nurse Hudson lapped her tongue over Annie's belly. She licked along the edge of her garter belt and probed her tongue-tip into Annie's navel. Annie giggled. Nurse Hudson giggled in reply.

"You're adorable," Nurse Hudson said.

Then her head moved down, her face sliding over Annie's belly to Annie's cunt. Leaning on her elbows, Annie looked down at the nurse's cap between her thighs. It seemed ridiculous to have a nurse's cap there.

Ridiculous or not, when Nurse Hudson's hands came around to spread open the lips of Annie's cunt, Annie vented a low, deep moan.

Nurse Hudson was obviously through wasting time. All the fondling and squeezing and tit sucking had been the appetizer for the main course. Now that the main dish in the feast was under her nose, Nurse Hudson moaned with delight. Her tongue came out of her mouth like a pink, wet snake and began a series of stabbing attacks at Annie's swollen clit.

Breathing heavily through her dry mouth, Annie managed to grunt at each touch of Nurse Hudson's agile tongue.

"Suck it!" Annie hissed. "Suck my pussy!"

She found it hard to believe the words were coming out of her mouth. Looking down, she could see Nurse Hudson's face buried in the curls of her cunt-mound. Nurse Hudson obviously loved sucking pussy. All the stories about her were absolutely true. Annie wondered how many other nurses had had their crotches cleaned out by Nurse Hudson's tongue!

Annie's swollen clit throbbed and quivered. A delicious warmth flowed out of her pussy to spread over her body. She no longer cared why she was there. She loved every moment of it!

Nurse Hudson knew that Annie no longer rejected her. She could tell by the relaxation of Annie's muscles and by the swelling of Annie's clit. When she exerted the slightest pressure on the insides of Annie's thighs, the younger nurse immediately opened her legs. Nurse Hudson worked her fingers down the hairy sides of her larger outer cunt-lips. She pried open Annie's luscious cunt and drilled her tongue deep into her soft, quivering cunt tunnel. Annie's cunt-juice oozed out like a flow of hot lava to cover Nurse Hudson's mouth. The older woman sucked and tasted her cunt-cream with a satisfied slurping noise. She stiffened her tongue and drove it deep into her cunt-hole. She pressed her nose against her enlarged clit. She thrilled at the fluttering reactions of Annie's meaty cunt-lips.

Nurse Hudson began opening the buttons of her uniform. Annie's eyes were closed and she was breathing rapidly through her mouth. Nurse Hudson's tongue continued working on Annie's drooling cunt. She kept her tongue in place even as she slipped out of her uniform mild unhooked her bra. She was soon naked from the waist up, her mammoth tits hanging like juicy melons. She continued licking and lapping every square inch of Annie's spread open cunt. She worked over her inner cuntlips. She drew her swollen clit into her mouth and carefully gripped it between her teeth.

Annie heaved up her thighs. A quivering moan of pleasure escaped her lips.

Working down, Nurse Hudson ran her stiff tongue deep into Annie's cunt-hole. She slobbered over the abundance of cunt-juice oozing out of her pussy. Continuing down further, she licked the smooth curves, at the junction of Annie's thighs and asscheeks. Annie groaned and pulled her legs back to expose more of her ass. Nurse Hudson spread Annie's asscheeks with her hands and gazed at the puckered ring of Annie's asshole. After nearly twenty years as a nurse, an asshole was not mysterious territory to Nurse Hudson. She'd had to cope with all kinds, all sizes, and all shapes. But this was not the asshole of some messy patient – this was the asshole of a beautiful young nurse! With an audible sigh, Nurse Hudson leaned forward and ran the very tip of her tongue over the wrinkled grommet of Annie's sweet little asshole.

"Oh, God!" Annie groaned.

Nurse Hudson wriggled a hand between her own thighs. Her fingers probed her crotch until she found the engorged shaft of her clit. Massaging her stiff clit, she continued licking Annie's asshole. Then she began pushing her tongue at her puckered anal-ring, demanding entrance. She continued to apply pressure until the muscle of her asshole relaxed and her tongue popped into her rubbery ass-channel. Like a tiny mouth, Annie's asshole closed and tightly gripped Nurse Hudson's tongue. When Nurse Hudson finally pulled out her tongue and straightened up, Annie's asshole flared out to protest the loss.

Using both hands, Nurse Hudson lifted one of her huge tits. Her stiff pink nipple was about the size of her thumb. Pressing forward, she brought her juicy teat up against the quivering meat of Annie's open cunt. She placed the nipple directly on Annie's clit. The full, hanging globe of her tit completely covered Annie's crotch!

One hand frantically playing with her own clit, Nurse Hudson vigorously massaged her tit over Annie's dripping cunt. Within moments, the older woman was gurgling and babbling in the throes of a stupendous climax. Annie stared wide-eyed as the Head Nurse quaked and groaned.

When Nurse Hudson's orgasm finally abated, she fell back in her chair and looked at Annie with glowing eyes.

"Come down here and suck my pussy," Nurse Hudson said.

Annie flushed scarlet. She hadn't expected that. She'd thought Nurse Hudson would do all the sucking. The idea of sucking another woman's cunt did not appeal to Annie at all. She'd never been able to understand how her boyfriends could enjoy putting their mouths on her dripping cunt. She tried keeping her pussy clean and fresh, but it was still a pussy. She had no idea about, the condition of Nurse Hudson's steaming crotch. Was she clean? Clean or not, Annie decided she really had no choice.

Nurse Hudson had all her clothes stripped off

now. She had a plump body. Her tits looked even more huge when she was completely naked. They hung down almost to her belly. Her large pink nipples were swollen and bloated with sexual arousal. Below the folds of Nurse Hudson's belly was a thick bush of auburn pubic hair. Annie stared at her protruding, tumescent cuntlips. Nurse Hudson's pink clit was stiff and throbbing.

For one terrifying moment, Annie felt that she couldn't do it. Then she remembered the power Nurse Hudson had over her – and with a sigh of resignation she slipped off the desk.

She knelt down between Nurse Hudson's legs. Sighing, Nurse Hudson smiled and raised one leg to more completely expose her gaping cunt.

"Do a good job," Nurse Hudson said. "I like it slow and easy. Have you ever done it before?"

Her eyes fixed on her steaming red cuntgash, Annie shook her head. "No," she said.

Nurse Hudson chuckled. "Well, there's always a first time, isn't there? Come on honey. Get that cute little tongue in my cunt and suck me out!"

Leaning forward, Annie rubbed her cheek against the warm insides of Nurse Hudson's thighs. She tasted the soft skin with her lips. She moved her face closer to the woman's cunt and sniffed. There was none of the intimate feminine smell she expected. There was nothing except the delicate aroma of new-mown hay, with maybe a hint of cinnamon, she couldn't tell. Whatever it was, it was pleasant. Using her fingers, Annie parted the thick, hairy outer lips of Nurse Hudson's cunt and placed her open mouth in the very centre of her juicy pussy-gash.

"That's it!" Nurse Hudson hissed. "Eat my pussy!"

Annie began kissing add licking Nurse Hudson's cunt. She found herself enjoying the softness of her pussy-flesh. She moved her pursed lips up and down her cunt-slit, savouring the feel of the rubbery, wet cunt-meat. She tickled her tongue-tip over her large clit – and then took it in between her lips and began sucking.

Nurse Hudson began gyrating her hips. She flexed her thighs and squirmed her ass. She held up a huge tit in each hand and whimpered.

"Oh, shit, yes!" she groaned. "Suck it, baby! Suck that box!"

Her body shuddering with one spasm after another, her cunt throbbed out its climax against Annie's tongue.

When it was over, Nurse Hudson looked down at Annie and patted her cheek.

"Thank you, darling," the older woman said, her voice aquiver with emotion. "That was so... beautiful!"

Annie said nothing. She felt ashamed and guilty, but at least, for the moment, her job was safe.

CHAPTER FIVE

The first time Annie heard about Jimmy Bell, she was sitting in the cafeteria eating her lunch and minding her own business. A nurse named Sophie Greensward sat down at Annie's table with a wink and a giggled.

"There's a monster in room 403," Sophie said.

Annie gave her a puzzled look. "Monster?"

Sophie nodded. "There's a teen-age kid in there with absolutely the biggest cock I've ever seen in my life."

Annie smiled and pushed away her salad. "Are you measuring them these days?"

"Don't be a smart-ass," Sophie giggled. "Go have a look and see for yourself. But keep your hands off, honey Hudson has been on the warpath for a week about nurses fooling around with patients. No cock in the world is worth trouble with Hudson."

Annie rolled her eyes and pretended to agree. She knew all about Head Nurse Hudson. After five days of sucking at Head Nurse Hudson's dripping pussy, there was nothing about Nurse Hudson Annie wasn't aware of.

Annie's poor little mouth was operating on a full schedule. She sucked off the Hospital Director every morning and the Head Nurse every afternoon. They'd promised her there would be only one more week of sucking, but the problem was whether Annie would last that long. It wasn't, the sucking that bothered her, it was the lack of variety. Peter Sikorski had a cute cock-head, but the man attached to the other, end of the cock was a clod. Head Nurse Hudson was a big-tittied bore. She'd made Annie suck on her fat nipples until Annie had a cramp in her jaw. All for the love of a stinking job! Annie's brain was getting rattled. She hadn't been near any man beside Peter Sikorski for nearly a week. Looking in on the patient in 403, just looking, would get her spirits up. Annie very badly wanted her spirits back up where they belonged.

The boy in 403 turned out to be a cute blond-haired, seventeen-year-old lad with freckles. His eyes lit up when Annie walked into the room with a friendly smile. He'd had a compound leg fracture. He had the leg in a cast, but otherwise he seemed fine. When Annie asked if he had any pain, he shook his head.

"I'm just bored," he said.

She sat down on the edge of the bed. She ruffled his blond curly hair. She questioned him about his leg and learned he'd broken it playing football.

"I bet your girlfriend misses you," she said.

He shrugged. "There's no one special."

Annie laughed. She squeezed the muscular thigh of his good leg. "Playing the field, huh? You must drive all the girls crazy."

His eyes were on the swell of her tits under her uniform. She ran her hand back and forth along his thigh. It wasn't long before she had her eyes fastened to the tent in the sheet produced by his obvious erection.

"Oh, wow!" she said with a smile. "Did I do that?"

Sighing, he nodded. He was evidently less naive than she'd assumed.

"I'm sorry," she said.

"It don't matter," he said. "It happens all the time."

"Uncomfortable?"

"Yeah," he said.

"Let's have a look."

She couldn't help it. After Sophie's rave introduction. Annie's curiosity had to be satisfied. She pulled down the sheet. She stared. She gasped!

"Oh, sweet Jesus!" she said.

A ten-inch horse-cock rose up out of his crotch like a baseball bat. She feasted her eyes on his thick white cock-shaft sprouting out of the sparse nest of blond hair between his strong thighs. His cock jerked and twitched. His heavy, hanging balls quivered. His bloated cock-head visibly swelled under her eyes.

"You're very... well built!" she said.

He looked bored. "Yeah," he said. "You wanna suck it?"

His boldness caught her by surprise. She wanted to get up and leave, but the sight of his huge cock held her back. "I don't think I ought to do that," she said. "But maybe I could... take care of it for you."

He snorted. "Sure," he said. "Whatever you want."

Extending a hand, she closed her fist around the shaft of his cock. He groaned. His pelvis rose up. His body jerked and twisted. She squeezed his throbbing cock-shaft in response. With a slow, leisurely stroke, she began masturbating him.

"I think this is the biggest one I've ever seen," she said.

"Do you like it?"

"It's lovely," she said.

She brushed the tips of her fingers against the silky flesh of his huge cock-knob. The heat of his cock-shaft under her hand was thrilling. She could hardly close her slender fingers around his fat cylinder of fuck-meat. He groaned and trembled as her fist moved up and down his throbbing prick. Her eyes glittering, she kept shifting her gaze from his contorted face to the red, angry-looking head of his gorgeous cock.

"Oh, shit!" he moaned. He squirmed his hips. His full, sleek-looking balls rolled back and forth. She used one hand to cup his balls and, the other hand to pump and stroke his prick-shaft.

"Feel good?" she asked. "Am I doing it right?"

A moment later, the first white pearls of hot jism came spurting out of the head of his cock like a geyser. Using both hands, she pressed down on the base of his convulsing prick-shaft.

"Oh, honey!" she crooned. "That's lovely! Keep coming! Give me all of it!"

As she watched his jism foam and spurt out of his bloated cock-head, she had a sudden urge to have her mouth stuffed with his cockmeat. Swooping down like a bird of prey, her jaws wide-open, she engulfed his spouting cock-head.

After days of the meagre rations of Peter Sikorski's sperm, the boy's thick, ropy cum was a welcome treat. Her lips glistening with jism, she pulled her mouth off his cock a moment.

"Delicious!" she said.

The boy groaned. The swollen, purplish head of his cock sent a thick set of white cockcream spurting against her face. His hot cum dripped down her cheeks and over her chin. With a soft moan, she jabbed the spitting head of his cock back into her mouth. She sucked and swallowed. Her hand worked up and down his throbbing cock-shaft to milk the last drop out of his balls.

"Oh, Jesus!" he groaned.

"Nice?"

"Yeah," he said.

His cock was still hard – not as stiff as before, but definitely not soft. She maintained her grasp on his cock. He was still trembling. When she pushed back his foreskin, the trembling increased. She chuckled at his excitement. She slid her hand down to his balls and began to play with them.

"They still look full," she teased. "Would you like to come again?"

He nodded. He gazed down at her hand as it

rubbed and fondled his balls.

"You just lie there and let me do the work," Annie said. She was dizzy with excitement. Her cunt was oozing a flood of cunt-juice between her thighs. She hadn't intended to fuck him, but the temptation was now too much to resist. She stroked his cock and gave it a playful squeeze. She ran a hand over the hard muscles of his belly. She smiled when he put his hand on her thigh.

"How many girls have you fucked?" she said.

He shrugged. "Jesus, I don't know," he said. "I don't count."

"Have you ever licked a pussy?"

He shook his head. "I've never done that," he said.

She pulled up her uniform. As usual, she was without panties and her pussy was bare. He stared fixedly at her luxuriant black bush of cunthair. She ran a hand between her legs and teased him by prying open her juicy pink cunt-lips. The hot glow in his eyes was delicious.

She climbed on the bed and kneeled beside him for a moment. Then she leaned forward and placed her hands on either side of his shoulders. She looked down into his eager, expectant young face. She threw a leg over his body and straddled him, moving her cunt over his head.

She had her uniform pulled up to her waist. He moved his hands around to cup her ass. He squeezed her asscheeks and pulled her crotch forward, into his face. His wet tongue swept through the fur covering her pussy. She felt the tip of his tongue flicking against her clit.

"That's good, honey," she said. "Just keep at it, you're doing fine."

He was an adorable kid. He ate her cunt slowly

and patiently. She thanked the woman brought him into the world. She hardly moved, except to let her right hand fall lightly on the top of his head. Her left hand continued to hold her uniform up out of the way. The hand on his head playfully ruffled his hair. She liked him. He wasn't afraid to push his nose deep and hard into a woman's vulva. He licked carefully, probing far with his tongue. She could feel her cunt become sopping wet with his saliva. She could feel his spit dribbling down her wet cunt-hair onto her inner thigh. It tickled a little, but she hardly noticed. Her thoughts were totally on the pleasure that danced along her engorged cunt lips, up to the straining nubbin of her clitoris, right to the very quick of her.

She finally pulled her cunt away from his mouth. She moved back to straddle his thighs. She positioned the hairy slot of her cunt over his massive fuck-meat. She reached down, took the red-knobbed cock in her hands, and centred it on her cunt-gash. Then she slowly squatted down until his fat cock-head touched her cunt-lips. She had cunt-juice oozing out of her pussy in a flood.

Christ, she thought. It's as big as the salami sausages hanging up in Mario's deli. She smeared some of it on the head of his cock. She rubbed his spongy cock-head up and down her cunt-slit, just barely touching her swollen clit. Then she squatted down, pushing his cock into her cunt, stuffing herself with its hot, throbbing hardness. A grunt of pleasure gurgled out of his throat.

She sat there a moment, her body speared on his cock. She straddled him as if he were a horse. She loved the feel of his huge young cock in her sopping wet cunt. She began grinding her hips, impaling herself on his cock and moaning her pleasure.

The boy grunted each time she completed a thrust on his cock. The look of pleasure on his face was exciting. She had him in her power. She felt herself to be in total control!

Now, she changed the movements of her hips to a slow, rhythmical hunching. He fucked his own hips up and down, pumping his cock in and out of her slippery cunt. The sounds of their groaning and grunting filled the room. Annie prayed no one out in the corridor could hear them. The danger of discovery increased her excitement. She frantically worked her hungry cunt up and down on the boy's giant cock. Her breathing was unsteady, her mouth gasping and sucking for air. She was now so excited, she was no longer aware of her surroundings. Having her cunt fully stretched by a thick cock always did this to her. No matter how strong her determination to maintain control, she sooner or later lost out to the pleasure of the fucking. Her eyes clamped shut for long moments, and then she opened them quickly as the rhythm of her fucking became frenzied.

She smiled at him. She reached a hand behind her and fingered his swollen balls. She shivered at the thought of his balls bloated with hot jism. She waited until he'd simmered down a little, and then she began pumping her cunt again. She moved slowly at first, and then with greater force and speed.

She was soon aware of the growing response of her body within moments, she was climbing up to an orgasm, shuddering and trembling ramming her cunt down oh the hot pole of his cock.

As she quaked and groaned through her climax,

his cock suddenly began spewing out its load. A torrent of sticky, hot jism flooded her cunt, shooting up her pussy channel in a foaming geyser. She cried out at the feel of it, gurgling and moaning with lust. Squeezed out by the spasms in bet cunt, her own cunt juice gushed down over his throbbing cock and drenched his balls.

With a final moan, she pulled the swollen flesh, of her cunt off his softening cock. His glistening fuck-meat popped out of her pussy hole and flopped on his thigh.

Annie gradually became aware of the time and place. She climbed off his body and left the bed. Holding her uniform up around the waist, she walked over to the small sink and briefly cleaned up her crotch. Then, she turned back to the bed. She looked down at the soft meat of his cock and smiled.

"You need cleaning, too," she said.

She had a sudden lecherous impulse to wash his cock and balls with her tongue. Why not? she thought. It's mostly my own cunt-juice. His flaccid cock lay on his thigh like a restless snake. Sitting on the edge of the bed, she lowered her fact toward his crotch.

Her nipples brushed his thighs. She took his cock in her hand, holding its weight on her palm. As she gazed at it, it began to swell and thicken. She watched the tip bloom and grow darker. She watched the soft skin grow tight and velvety before her eyes. She felt the thickness of him in her hand. His cock pulsed with an animal power under her fingers as his blood pumped into it. She watched his balls jerking up and down in their wrinkled sac.

She had no doubt that she'd be able to make him come again. This would be the third time. Maybe afterward he'd be able to get some rest! A shiver went down her spine at the lewdness of what she was doing. It certainly wasn't the accepted way to wash up a patient! Her pussy quivered. She could feel her cunt-lips swelling up again.

He was now pumping his hips at her, making his cock slide in her hand. She tipped his cock-shaft toward her mouth. Opening her lips, she sucked him in.

"Oh, Christ!" he moaned.

His cock filled her mouth, pushing her tongue aside and bloating out her cheeks. She could taste herself somewhere in the flavor of his juice-coated fuck-meat. She took his cock all the way in until his velvety cock-head hit the back of her throat. She made a mewling sound of pleasure and went to work on him.

She licked and sucked until all the flavor of their combined juices was gone. Then she pulled her mouth off his cock and licked along the root of his cock-shaft. Her tongue lashed out again and again, her lips sucking and kissing with a loud wet noise.

She followed her nose into the bush of his crotch-hair. She washed her tongue over the folded, wrinkled skin of his balls. When she stuffed his glistening cock back into her mouth, he pushed his hips up toward her face.

"Oh, yeah!" he moaned. "Oh, Christ, that's good!"

She felt his cock swell and tremble and push back to her throat. She knew he'd come soon! She tightened her lips and increased the suction on his cock-head. A moment later, his fat cock-knob swelled up like a balloon and throbbed out the first jet of his milky jism. The salvo of sperm surged past her lips, over the flat of her tongue and into her throat. She felt the warm, slippery splatter of his cock-cream trickling down her gullet. She heard him groan. His hands grabbed her head. His hips writhed beneath her face. She kept sucking until the flow stopped, and then she squeezed his balls and sucked some more.

He groaned. She finally pulled her mouth off his cock with a slurping noise. She swirled her tongue over her lips and swallowed the clinging remnants of his cum.

"Enough?"

"Jesus, yeah!" he said.

She playfully pinched his cock and pulled up the sheet to cover him. Tweaking his nose, she turned on her heel and pranced out of the room.

CHAPTER SIX

"You've been avoiding me," Grant Silvers said.

Stretched out like a lazy cat, Annie watched the young intern move slowly toward the bed. Grant Silvers was the second man in her life. In the end, it would be either Jake or Grant. Sometime soon she would have to make a decision – assuming, of course, she didn't murder Nurse Hudson and wind up in jail.

Her eyes caressed the muscular strength of Grant's naked body. He approached her with his gaze fixed between her outstretched legs. His heavy cock touched her thigh as he positioned himself beside her on the bed. His hands moved to her tits. His touch was light and knowing. Her nipples immediately responded, hardening and throbbing with desire. She leaned into his gently massaging fingers. A contented purring sound escaped from her lips.

The corners of her mouth turning up in a soft smile, she slipped a hand down to his crotch and took his cock between her fingers. Her hand gradually tightened around his thick cock-shaft.

"Yeah, baby," he said. "That feels nice." With a short grunt, he pushed his fuck-meat into her clutching fingers.

Annie ran the ball of her thumb over the smooth, tight skin of his cock-head. She dabbed at the fluid welling out of his cock-slit and spread it over the surface of his spongy cock-knob. She ran her fingertips up and down his fat, pulsing shaft, tracing out the network of thick veins. The one certain thing about Grant Silvers was that he had an impressive cock.

She suddenly gasped at the touch of Grant's hot, wet mouth on the hard nipple of her right tit. His tongue lashed out to caress her long, sensitive nipple-tip. She could feel the sharp edges of his teeth tightening on her nipple. She pushed her tit against his face and moaned.

"That's it!" she said. "Suck it!"

She moved a hand to the back of his head and pulled his face into her tit-flesh. The harder he sucked on her nipple, the harder she pumped on his cock. He began humping his ass, fucking his throbbing cock in and out of her hand. She could feel his steaming cockhead pressing against the side of her body. Her eyes clamped shut. She shivered at the exquisite sensation produced by his mouth on her swollen nipple.

She rolled on her side to make it easier for him

to play with her tits. The palm of her hand rubbed against the bloated head of his cock. Her other hand continued pumping the full length of his pulsing cock-shaft. She moved the tip of his cock to the hairy mound of her cunt. She could feel the wetness between her legs. She could feel the soft, wet lips of her pussy kissing his swollen cock. She fitted his fat cock-head to the mouth of her cunt and their bodies began moving in rhythm.

She suddenly snapped back her hips, pulling her wet cunt off of his cock. "Not yet," she said. "Eat me first. Suck my pussy before we fuck!"

Grant looked at her and grinned. "You're a hot-assed bitch, aren't you?" he said. He began sliding down the front of her body. The coolness of the air-conditioned hospital room brought a quiver to the nipples of her trembling tits. Grant's long, hot tongue left a wet trail across her belly. His face was soon poised over the steaming gulch of her sweet-smelling cunt. His strong fingers held her fleshy thighs. Lewdly smacking his lips, he pressed his face into the hairy dampness of her crotch.

"Suck me!" Annie hissed. She rammed her cunt against his handsome mouth.

He moved his hands behind her to cup her asscheeks. He rolled her over onto her back. She wrapped her legs around his neck and drove her heels against his shoulder blades. She babbled and mewled as his tongue toyed with her stiff clit. He moved his tongue down to probe the deep cavern of her dripping cunt. Annie moaned when she felt the warm muscle of his tongue pistoning in and out of her cunt-hole like a small cock.

"Oh, Jesus!" she cried. "I love that! Fuck me with your tongue!"

His fingers massaged the heavy globes of her ass, pulling her body up to meet each new thrust. She tossed her head and rocked her body from side to side. Shivers of excitement surged through her body when she felt his fingertips creeping into the deep crack between her asscheeks. She gasped when he began playing with the tight muscular ring of her asshole. With a sudden, growl of passion, she pushed him away and forced him to stretch out on his back.

Grant grinned. "You're the boss," he said. He knew she'd bring him to the very peak of excitement and then drain every drop of jism out of his balls. He folded the pillow under his head. His eyes raked up and down the length of her body.

Sighing, Annie leaned over him. Her heavy tits fell forward, her long, dark nipples swaying, over his chest.

"Stick out your tongue," she giggled.

When his red, pulpy tongue obediently came out of his mouth, she dropped her spongy nipple onto its wet surface. She teased him with one tit and then the other until both her nipples glistened with his saliva. She kept her right hand working up and down on his thick cock. Once again, Grant moved a hand to her ass and tickled her asshole. She kissed him and sucked his tongue into her mouth. Then he pulled her face away and her wet lips and tongue caressed his neck. She was soon working her mouth over his shoulders and hairy chest. Wrapping her lips around one of his tiny nipples she sucked at it as she squirmed down the length of his body.

She rested the side of her face against his hard belly and pressed the thick shaft of his cock into her tits. Her tongue probed his navel. She rolled his hot cock against her sweaty flesh. Moving her face farther down, she poised her mouth over, his swollen, throbbing cock-head.

"Suck it!" he hissed. "Come on, baby! Get it in there and suck it!"

Extending her tongue out as far as possible, she began licking the full length of his fuckmeat. She licked up and down, from the base of his cock to the tiny slit at the tip of his bulging cock-head. She slurped and slobbered over every inch of his quivering pink cock-meat.

Her mouth soon worked its way down to his heavy balls. Opening her jaws wide, she sucked first one and then the other ball into her mouth and rolled it on her tongue. She popped his balls out of her mouth and pushed his knees back to tilt up his crotch. A low pitched groan escaped Grant's throat as the tip of her tongue found the tight puckered ring of his asshole. His thighs tensed and jerked. Her face pressed into the crack of his ass, Annie pushed her tongue forward into the steaming depths of his asshole.

The drilling of her warm tongue into his ass soon had him bucking and groaning like a wild animal. She pulled away as soon as she realized he was close to coming. Scrambling off to the side, she positioned herself on her hands and knees. She leaned forward with her face and tits on the bed and her ass in the air. Her shoulders carrying her weight in front, she reached behind her back and pried open her plump asscheeks.

"Fuck me, honey!" she hissed. "Fuck my ass!"

Filling his hands with her rubbery asscheeks, lifting her hips, he positioned himself behind her and poked the head of his cock at her tiny asshole. His cock was sufficiently lubricated from her sucking. Prying open her asshole, he succeeded in pushing in first the tip of his cock, then the whole head – then most of the shaft! Annie groaned. Grant had a big cock, and the feel of it reaming out her ass always drove her wild. She felt like a bug impaled on a pin. The feel of his fuck-muscle violating her tight ass was exquisite.

Grant was soon thrusting vigorously in and out of her loosened, pinky-brown asshole. Pummelling the attractive nurse's ass whenever they had a bat session was always a treat. Of all the women he fucked, Annie had the most educated asshole. She knew exactly when to squeeze down on his cock to increase his pleasure. He loved the super-tight clutch of her hot asshole as it gripped his probing cock-meat.

Annie felt as if someone were shooting a deliciously hot blowtorch up her ass. She mewled and squirmed. For one crazy moment, she imagined Grant was a thoroughbred stallion fucking her with a horse-cock! She bucked her ass against his powerful thrusts. She gasped and sobbed as she moved up to an intense orgasm.

"Oh, sweet Jesus, fuck my ass," she groaned. "Fuck me hard!"

The exquisite spasms of her orgasm racked her body. Moments later, Grant vented a series of grunts and began squirting his thick jism up the chute of her ass.

They finally rolled away from each other and collapsed on the bed – exhausted.

An hour later, Annie grabbed a quick shower in the surgery wing in preparation for her daily session with Peter Sikorski. She wasn't mean enough, to go to Sikorski with her two holes greased by another man's cum. After reaming out her ass, Grant had fucked her pussy ragged. He'd left her with a crotch full of his jism, a stretched out cunt, and a sore asshole. She felt better after the shower, but she still had a fucked-out feeling in her crotch and she had to walk a little bowlegged.

Sikorski leered, smiled and took her hand.

"You look radiant," he said.

"I feel fine," Annie said. She wanted to tell him he was a damn hypocrite. He really didn't care how she felt or looked. All he cared about was getting his wrinkled old balls emptied out!

He locked the office door and turned off all the lights except a small table lamp. As usual, he immediately approached her and put his hands on her tits.

"How's my little sexpot?" he leered.

His fingers opened the buttons of her uniform. He helped her slip out of her dress and draped it over a chair. He unhooked her bra. He weighed her tits in his hands like a man buying melons at a fruit stand. He fastened his mouth on one of her long, hard nipples and sucked at it hungrily.

As far as Annie was concerned, the exasperating thing about these sessions was that he somehow always managed to turn her on. She wanted to remain as cold as ice – but her body always deceived her!

He pulled his mouth off her tit and smiled. "I bet you can get one in your mouth," he said.

"What?"

"I bet you can get a nipple in your mouth. Try it. Let's see if you can do it."

Her pussy quivered. Shivering with lust, she raised up a tit with both hands. By extending her tongue out as far as possible, she just managed to lick her swollen nipple.

"Beautiful!" Sikorski said. "Now, that turns me on!"

She knew what was coming next. They'd been through the routine before. He sometimes had a crazy passion to watch her masturbate. She never minded doing that in front of a man, as long as there was fucking afterward. Sikorski, however, sometimes did no more than jerk off on her tits or cunt. She considered that a waste. She liked the feel of a man fucking his jism into her body. Watching his cock squirt out his cum was nice, but only second best.

She slid a hand down to her crotch and fingered her cunt-lips. Sikorski's eyes glittered when she pushed two fingers into the grip of her cunt-hole. She pulled her fingers out and held them up to show him the coating of cuntjuice.

"Wet little hole, baby?" he grinned.

She nodded. Her cunt was dripping wet. There was no way to pretend it wasn't!

"Fuck it a little," he said. "Use your fingers like a cock."

She began ramming her fingers in and out of her cunt-hole. His hands fumbled with his belt and fly. He eventually freed his swollen cock and began slowly stroking it with his fist. Annie stared at his huge cock-head and thought about how it would feel inside her dripping cunt.

A moment later, too close to coming, he stopped jerking off and started mauling her tits again. He sucked her nipples like a wild animal. She thrust her tits up at his face. She liked the way he squeezed and pulled on them. She knew they'd be sore afterward, but at the moment she wanted his fingers digging in. It was strange how now that she was on the receiving end, she liked a little pain. Arching her back, she focused her attention on the sensations in her tits.

He had a tit in each hand, and he squeezed until her soft tit-flesh bulged out around his fingers. He grabbed her long nipples with his thumbs and forefingers. He pulled her tits out from her chest as far as they would stretch. He twisted and pinched her swollen nipples to produce an exquisite combination of pain and pleasure. The muscles of her belly quivered out of control. Her crotch was saturated with the gushing juices from her cunt.

"Get on the sofa!" he hissed.

He made her stretch out with her legs splayed wide-open to show her cunt. Kneeling between her feet, he pulled her cunt-lips open with both hands.

"Christ, what a cunt!" he said. "You're like an animal in heat! Your cunt is like a furnace!"

She moaned and wiggled her ass. He continued pulling out her cunt-lips. She looked down and saw the amazing length to which he had drawn out her pussy-flesh.

He finally released her and slipped his trousers down to free his cock and balls. His fat pink cock stood straight out from his body, his cock-head bloated and dripping. He crawled between her legs. She was aware of nothing else but her incredible need to be fucked. She was thankful he got on with it. He positioned his cock-head at the mouth of her cunt, grabbed the cheeks of her ass, and slammed his hard hot cock in to the hilt.

"Oh, God, yes!" she groaned. "Fuck me!" Supporting her ass with his hands, he balanced himself on his knees. He began to fuck her with a tough, relentless, thrusting of his hips. Annie was surprised that a man his age could be so physically active. Without any letup, he continued fucking her as hard as any of the younger men she knew. When she began groaning, he pulled his lips back on his teeth and grinned.

"You like it, huh? You thought old Sikorski couldn't cut the mustard, didn't you?"

She slammed her cunt up to meet each powerful thrust. She cried and whimpered when he suddenly pulled his cock out of her cunt and leered down at her.

"Not yet," he said. "It's not that easy."

Moving a hand to her cunt, he pinched her throbbing clit between two fingers. She wailed and threw her ass high off the sofa. Keeping his fingers on her clit, he used his other hand to probe her sopping wet cunt-hole. He soon had three fingers pistoning in and out of the steaming channel of her cunt.

"You've got a great little box," he said.

Then he giggled. "It's easy to understand why Head Nurse Hudson enjoys chewing on it. When was the last time Hudson went down on you?"

Annie moaned. "Yesterday."

"Did you like it?"

She moaned again. "Oh, God, I can't talk about that now! Fuck me! For God's sake, do something!"

His head suddenly swooped down, his sucking mouth searching out her cunt. She cried out and bucked her wet pussy up at his face. When she felt his hard finger pushing against her asshole, she knew it was only a matter of time before he blew her mind with a fantastic orgasm.

There was nothing delicate about the way he used his finger in her ass – he rammed it in deep, fucked it around, and made sure to let her know it was there.

She strained her cunt against his face and clutched at his finger with her asshole. She soon found herself in the midst of a fantastic orgasm. Her hands grabbed at his head as she tried to force his face into her crotch. He pulled away with a laugh and locked down at her. He kept pistoning his finger in and out of her asshole and grinning at the way she bucked up each time to meet it.

"You like having your sweet little shit-hole reamed out, don't you honey?"

She closed her eyes and whimpered. "Please! Oh, jeez, yes *please!*"

There was a sudden stretching of her asshole and she realized he now had two fingers inside. She groaned and kept bucking her ass against his hand. She had her own fingers massaging her clit, pulling and tugging at the sensitive nub of flesh in rhythm with his fingers fucking her ass.

There was a sudden sharp pain in her ass as he pushed in a third finger. The pain lasted no more than a moment and, then began the most intensely pleasurable sensation she had ever experienced! The pleasure rose up in a series of crescendos. The last thing she saw before oblivion was Sikorski drooling at the mouth as he watched his three fingers pumping in and out of her stretched asshole.

CHAPTER SEVEN

Annie sat on the toilet idly fingering the lips of her pussy and thinking about John Hacker. More than a week had passed since his discharge from the hospital, and now he'd invited her to party at his apartment. She was eagerly looking forward to an evening of fun. The people at the hospital had been getting on her nerves, particularly Head Nurse Hudson and Doctor Sikorski, and it would be good to get out for a carefree evening.

In the meantime, it couldn't do any harm to warm up a little. She sat on the toilet with her legs wide apart. She rubbed her middle finger up and down the groove of her pussy. The fed of her fingertip moving along the trail from clit to cunt-hole and back again was delicious.

She closed her eyes and thought about John Hacker. She thought about socking his cock. She thought about his mouth on her cunt. She thought about his cock in her ass. She kept moving her finger from the mouth of her cunt to her clit, repeating the stroke over and over.

It was really silly the way women were constructed – she could never understand why her clit wasn't inside her cunt-hole where it belonged.

She soon added a second finger to the first. One finger was fine, but she liked stretching the mouth of her cunt-hole. Her pussy responded with a delicate quiver at the entry of the second intruder.

She concentrated more intently on the idea Hacker eating her and then fucking her. She used her thumb now, together with her two plunging fingers. She deftly pinched her clit each time she pushed her fingers into the hot grip of her cunt-hole. She twisted her ass on the toilet. Cunt-juice oozed out of her cunt to drip off her pistoning fingers into the water.

"Oh, shit!" she groaned. "This is crazy!"

But there was no way she could stop now. She stroked herself more vigorously. Her eyes tightly shut, she imagined the feeling of a hard cock plunging in and out of her cunt. She drew closer and closer to the climax, and then, finally, the tremors were rolling up through her belly and she moaned out her release.

She felt better now. She felt more ready for John Hacker's party. By the time she got out of the bathroom, her only thoughts concerned the clothes she would wear.

Hacker met her at the door with a drink in his hand and a smile on his face. He had lipstick on his cheek. His tie was loose and he looked happy.

"Come join the party," he said.

It turned out Hacker's idea of a party was three people – himself, Annie, and another woman.

Her name was Daphne. She had dark hair, dark eyes, and a slim body sheathed in a slinky dress. She looked about the same age as Annie.

Hacker mixed Annie a drink and they all sat and chatted to get better acquainted. Annie had no doubts about Hacker's intentions – he wanted both women, either one after the other or at the same time. She had to admire his nerve. She'd never been involved in a threesome before, and she found herself ready and willing to try it. Daphne obviously had no qualms about it either – her mouth was soon locked with Hacker's in a wet kiss, and a moment later her hand was fondling his huge erection.

Annie shivered at the lewd sight of Daphne's hand on Hacker's meaty cock. Hacker's hands were on Daphne's thrusting tits. Daphne continued to stroke his hard cock. His long thick cock-shaft looked very white, and Annie could see his bulging cock head, red and shiny, as Daphne's hand moved over it.

Daphne finally pulled her lips away from Hacker's mouth. Her hand still holding his cock, she looked at Annie and smiled.

"John told me you and this salami of his are old friends. I hope you don't mind."

Annie shrugged. She was feeling the effects of the liquor. She certainly didn't mind that Daphne knew that she and Hacker had fucked. At the moment, Annie was more interested in how public Daphne wanted things.

Daphne evidently wanted things very public, indeed! She slipped off the couch and knelt on the floor between Hacker's legs. Annie's heart raced as she watched the elegant brunette run her pink tongue over the swollen head of Hacker's huge cock. Hacker slumped back against the soft cushions of the sofa. His eyes were half-closed. His lips were turned up in a smile as he watched Daphne's mouth working on his fuck-meat.

Annie stared transfixed at the scene. She watched Daphne lick his huge cock while her hand moved possessively up and down his long cock-shaft. Daphne opened her mouth. She swooped down and half the length of his cock disappeared between her lips.

Hacker's body stiffened as the brunette's mouth moved steadily up and down over his bulging cock-head. He vented a deep groan of pleasure and grabbed Daphne's head with his hands to direct the rhythm of her sucking.

Annie was very much aware of her own excitement. She had a hand between her legs, continually rubbing her burning crotch through the material of her dress. She kept her eyes locked on the stretched lips of Daphne's mouth moving up and down on his long shaft of glistening cock-meat. The lewdness of it all was too much to bear. Slipping a hand under her dress, Annie began directly massaging her cunt with her fingers. She couldn't remember the last time she'd been so turned on. She had a flood of cunt-juice flowing out her cunt and her knees were quivering.

Daphne suddenly pulled her mouth off Hacker's cock. She rose up and began a slow dance around the room. Her hands fluttering over her body, she stripped off her clothes piece by piece. She was soon wearing nothing more than, a flimsy garter belt to hold up her nylons. She had drooping, pear-shaped tits with long, brown nipples, a curvy, firm looking ass, and a dense bush of dark cunt hair below her belly.

Hacker caught Annie's eye and grinned. "Come on over here and get cozy," he said.

Annie rose up and walked across the room. She was conscious of their eyes on her body. She knelt down between Hacker's legs. His cock had softened up a bit, but it was still long enough to bring a flutter to her pussy. She held his limp cock-shaft in her hand. His bare cock-head had a dull, purplish-pink color. Extending her wet tongue, Annie began licking his prick.

She swirled her tongue over his velvety, mushroom-shaped cock-knob. The knowledge that another woman was watching her doing it made it all the more exciting. Opening her mouth wide, she engulfed his entire cock, taking all of him until his fat cock head jammed into the back of her throat and the tight ring of her lips pressed against his shorts. When she pulled back her mouth, she let her saliva drool down to bathe his swollen cock-meat.

She began steadily pumping her mouth up and down on his cock, slurping and slobbering over his thick cylinder of rampant prick-flesh, fucking him with her face and shivering at the obscene picture she knew she was making. She sucked hard on his cock-head each time she drew back, and then on the downstroke she let his cock-head slide over her tongue as the ring of her lips moved down to the base of his cockshaft. She finally had him stiffened out again, his cock long and hard, her mouth filled with his spongy cock-knob. She concentrated all her attention on twisting and pumping her mouth, sucking him furiously until he vented a hoarse groan. He slid his hands into her hair and caressed her head as it bobbed up and down on his fleshy prick.

"Oh, yeah, that's nice!" Hacker growled. "How does it taste, baby?"

Annie pulled her mouth off his cock and smiled. "Delicious!" she said. She turned and looked at Daphne. The other woman was standing nearby, her legs wide apart, her hand massaging her cunt as she watched Annie work on Hacker.

Moving her mouth back to Hacker's cock, Annie extended her tongue and swirled it over his spongy cock. His bloated cock-head wobbled back and forth on its supple stalk. She held his cock-shaft near the base. She licked the underside of his cock-tip, then slid her tongue in the groove behind the flared rim of his cock-head. His cock-knob bobbed and weaved. She took his cock-tip between her lips again, and slid the ring of her mouth down towards, the base. She had nearly all of his cock inside her mouth. Her cheeks alternately hollowed, and swelled as she sucked his meaty prick.

Hacker's cock was soon as hard as iron. She had to withdraw until she held little more than his cock-head inside her mouth. She sucked on his cock-knob and massaged the underside with her tongue. When she finally pulled her mouth away with a slurping noise, Daphne hissed.

"Let me have a turn at that."

Annie shifted her body to the side and Daphne knelt down beside her. Shivering with lust, Annie kept her hand at the base of Hacker's cock and offered his fuck-meat to Daphne's mouth.

Opening her mouth wide, Daphne engulfed his fat cock-head and began bobbing her head up and down with a rapid, slurping rhythm. Annie finally pulled her hand away and rose up to her feet. She stripped off her clothes. She kept her eyes fixed on the curve of Daphne's naked ass. With an amused gleam in her eyes, she took a step back and peered down to catch a glimpse of Daphne's asshole. John noticed what she was looking at and laughed. Daphne pulled her mouth off his cock and turned up at puzzled glance.

"It's nothing," Hacker grinned. "Annie's looking at your ass. Maybe it's because she's a nurse."

Daphne chuckled. "Do I pass inspection?" Annie blushed. "Sorry," she said. "Next time I won't be so obvious." She decided it was time to get her clothes off. Daphne heartily approved and clapped her hands when Annie unhooked her bra to reveal her heavy tits.

"It's about time," Daphne said.

Annie laughed. She posed for them, turning her body to show her ass and tits. She saw them whispering together and wondered what was going on. Hacker finally grinned and spoke.

"Daphne needs a favour," he said. "She's never had it in the ass. She wants you to hold her hand while I try it."

Annie looked at Daphne. Daphne blushed. "I thought you might help," Daphne said. "He said he did it to you, and... well... you're a nurse, aren't you? I mean if anything goes wrong, you're right here!"

Annie giggled. Hacker suggested they go to the bedroom. "The floor's too hard on the knees," he said. They walked off to the bedroom, the two naked women on either side of Hacker, helping, him remove his clothes.

Daphne quickly arranged Hacker on the bed and dived down to stuff her mouth with his cock. Sitting up against the headboard, Hacker fondled her ears to encourage the sucking.

Annie climbed on the bed and crouched behind Daphne. She feasted her eyes on the full curves of Daphne's ass. Part of Daphne's cunt and all of her asshole was clearly visible. Daphne was hairy. Dark curls ran from Daphne's pussy into the crack of her ass and around her asshole. At first Annie just looked. Then she ran her fingertips over the full curves of Daphne's luscious ass. Her hand moved down to the pouting lips of Daphne's cunt. She fluttered her fingers over her thick, drooping cunt-lips and finally probed between them to find some cunt-juice.

Scooping out some of Daphne's cunt cream, Annie carried it up to the girl's tiny, hair-rimmed asshole. She smeared the pussy juice into her puckered, muscular anal-ring.

Her mouth filled with Hacker's cock, Daphne stifled a groan and lurched forward under the probing caress of Annie's finger in her ass. Annie began finger-fucking Daphne's sweet little asshole to the same rhythm as the brunette's sucking of Hacker's cock. Annie tilted her head to the side to study the hang of Daphne's long-nippled breasts. Extending her hand, Annie ran it over Daphne's jiggling tits. She pulled and pinched her fruity nipples until Daphne squealed.

Daphne suddenly pulled her mouth off Hacker's cock. "I need fucking!" she groaned.

She rolled over on her back and pulled her knees up to her chest. Her meaty cunt lay upturned and waiting, her pussy flaps in gleaming disarray. Hacker moved above her and, sliding his cock head through her juicy labia, rested it at the mouth of her cunt for a few moments, then plunged in with a single, smooth stroke.

"Oh, Jeez, yes!" Daphne moaned.

Hacker's balls slapped heavily against her ass. Annie watched them fuck with a hand busy at her own cunt. On a sudden impulse, she extended her free hand and grabbed Hacker's swinging balls from underneath his ass. He had full, heavy balls. The feel of them jiggling was delicious. She ran the tip of her thumb over his hairy asshole, and then pushed the digit inside the tight ring of his asshole.

Hacker grunted. Flexing his asscheeks, he tightened his ring on Annie's finger, finally pulling his cock out of Daphne's cunt and growling.

"Get on your hands and knees," he said. "Show me your ass!"

Moaning softly, Daphne crouched on her knees with her head down and her ass in the air. She turned her face and looked at Annie with glazed eyes.

"Don't let him hurt me," Daphne pleaded. Annie smiled and patted Daphne's ass affectionately. "Don't worry, honey," she said, then giggled. "I'm a nurse, remember? I'll get some Vaseline and loosen you up first."

Returning from the bathroom with a jar of Vaseline, it occurred to Annie that Daphne was fortunate to have another woman around to help. If it wasn't done right, getting fucked in the ass for the first time could be a horrible experience. Most men become too excited to use the necessary caution.

A huge grin on his face, Hacker stepped aside to let Annie grease up Daphne's tender asshole.

Annie ran her fingers over her firm asscheeks in her palms, squeezed and fondled them, and finally spread them open to feast her eyes.

The tight wrinkled pucker of Daphne's asshole winked up at her. Below it, the plump outer lips of Daphne's pussy bulged and pouted. Her pink tender inner lips were unfurled and hanging down. It was a lusty, meaty looking cunt. Scooping up some Vaseline on her thumb, Annie began massaging Daphne's tight asshole.

Daphne vented a soft moan. "Oh, sweet Jesus!" she said, "that's soooo nice. I always like being touched there."

Daphne's asshole looked hardly big enough to take a cock, but Annie was able to work her thumb inside without any difficulty.

The only response out of Daphne was a grunt of pleasure. Annie now began massaging the inside of Daphne's asshole, pulling and stretching the ring of muscle until it loosened up and lost its tension. Pulling out her thumb, Annie replaced it with her middle finger. She reamed out her asshole with a screwing motion, and then she added her forefinger to the middle finger, opening out both fingers like a pair of scissors, to stretch out her asshole farther.

A deep groan rumbled out of Daphne's throat. Annie looked at Hacker and saw that he'd already greased up his cock.

"I think we're ready," Annie said, catching Hacker's eye with a bright smile.

She fingered Hacker's cock, pinched his fat swollen cock-head, and squeezed a gob of precum out of his cock-slit. Then she positioned his cock-head at the ring of Daphne's asshole.

"Open up, honey," Annie said. "Just relax your muscles. There'll be a little pain at first, but it doesn't last. Just bear down, you know, push hard, like you're trying to take a really big, satisfying dump. Only – please don't do it for real."

Grunting like an animal, his hands clutching the globes of Daphne's ass, Hacker pushed forward. Annie could see the tight ring of the girl's ass opening up as he drove his cock into her. He moved forward with a series of short, powerful thrusts, forcing the head of his cock into her tight asshole like a pile driver. Daphne whimpered with each forward jab. Her eyes glazed over with fascination, Annie watched the girl's asshole stretch like rubber to accept his throbbing cock.

The walls of Daphne's ass channel clutched and

pulled at the fleshy foreskin of Hacker's cock. He rammed his cock in until he had his wiry crotch-hair pressing against her ass.

"Oh, fuck!" she mewled. "Oh, sweet mercy!"

She began grinding her ass in frenzy, urging him to fuck her. Smiling, Annie watched his greasy cock pistoning in and out of Daphne's elastic asshole. She patted Hacker's ass. She fondled his swinging balls. Climbing on the bed, Annie opened her thighs in front of Daphne's face and pulled the girl's mouth down to her dripping cunt.

Soon she felt the girl's tongue on her pussy, travelling all over her excited labia and clit in wild, random sweeps. She tightened her grip on the girl's head, her fingers enmeshed in Daphne's hair and bucked her pelvis upwards to increase the contact. Hacker was close to coming. Annie imagined him shooting the contents of his testicles into Daphne's ass cavity, coating the insides of her rectum with a flood of thick, white sperm. She started to shake and buck as the other girl's tongue relentlessly lapped and slurped her clitoral bean. Finally it arrived... a gigantic orgasm picked her up and shook her like a rag doll. She felt as if she were losing control... of everything. A thick, clear ejaculate gushed out of her pussy with such force, that much of it filled Daphne's eager mouth and soaked her upturned features. Annie was disconcerted, not to say a little embarrassed. Nothing like this had ever happened before. But to her great relief, a shiny-faced Daphne simply straightened up, smiled and said, "Mmmm... you taste wonderful, Nurse. You can squirt in my mouth any time."

At that point, Hacker felt a sudden tickle that

started somewhere in the depths of his big, ovoid balls and, travelling up the length of his thick cock, was met by an intense sensation of agonising pleasure travelling in the opposite direction from the tip of his shaft. He gasped and whimpered as his body was wracked with spasm after spasm of delicious orgasm and shot his hot, viscous load into the clinging, buttery depths of her shit tube, triggering Daphne's own violent orgasm. The trio collapsed, exhausted, on the bed. Annie watched Hacker's cock slip out of Daphne's hairy asshole with a soft little sigh, releasing a small gush of pearly jism that trickled slowly down the curve of her asscheek.

CHAPTER EIGHT

Stretched out on the sofa, one leg rocking to the rhythm of the music on the stereo Annie leisurely sucked oh Peter Sikorski's balls. She gently rolled his balls from one side of her mouth to the other. She popped them out of her lips, and began licking his wrinkled ballsac with her tongue. Wearing only his shirt and tie, one foot raised up on the sofa cushion to make room for Annie's head, Sikorski sighed.

"You're very good at that," he said.

Annie purred. She'd come to like Sikorski. He really wasn't a bad guy. Sometimes she thought of him as a father-figure. There was something definitely erotic about lying there sucking the balls of a man his age. His ball-sac was loose enough so that she could really get his balls toward the back of her throat. She liked that. She had fantasies about swallowing his balls. She imagined what the newspapers would make of that – nurse castrates Hospital Director. But the difficulty with swallowing his balls was that they'd no longer be there to suck on. Annie liked sucking balls. She liked sucking Sikorski's balls best of all! Maybe it was because it turned him into a lamb. It seemed that every time she had his balls in her mouth, he became docile and affectionate. He was really just like her father. She'd never, of course, had her father's balls in her mouth – but she imagined this was what it would be like!

"I've invited Tim Fenton here this evening," Sikorski said.

Coughing and sputtering, Annie spit out Sikorski's balls and looked up at him in astonishment.

"There, there," Sikorski said. "Don't be so upset." He tried pushing his cock-head into Annie's mouth. Some pre-cum dripped out of his cock-slit and covered one of her eyebrows. She pushed his cock away from her lips and looked hurt.

"But, Peter," she whimpered, "if Tim Fenton sees me here, he'll know something is going on."

Sikorski chuckled. "He already knows, my pet. Think of it as a favour. Tim Fenton is the best surgeon we have at the hospital, isn't he?"

"Yes," Annie said. "He certainly is."

"And we wouldn't want to lose him, would we?"

"No," Annie said. "We certainly wouldn't."

"Well, Tim has been depressed since his divorce and I think we ought to bring him out of it. Just think of it as a favor to good old Clinton Peak Hospital. You're loyal to the hospital, aren't you?"

"Yes, I am," Annie said.

"Good," Sikorski sighed. "Then it's settled. Tonight, we'll transform Tim Fenton into a happy man! Doesn't that sound nice?"

"Yes," Annie said.

"What are you wearing under that dress? You've been here nearly an hour and I haven't had a look at you yet."

Annie pulled her dress up over her thighs and exposed her bare pussy. It never made sense to wear panties when she visited Sikorski. He's sooner or later tear them off. She let her legs fall open to give him a good look at her cunt.

"Delicious!" Sikorski said. "I think we're going to make Tim very happy tonight."

Annie was hoping Sikorski would take time out for a few laps at her pussy. Sucking his balls had juiced up her cunt, and Sikorski had demonstrated more than once that he had an expert tongue and enjoyed using it. There was nothing that turned Annie on more than a man who liked sucking pussy – and knew how to do it?

Unfortunately, Sikorski's mind was occupied with Tim Fenton. "We're going out to dinner," Sikorski said. "I think I'd better get my clothes on. Tim has to be sort of led into things, you know. I've always had the impression he's a little bit of a prude."

When Fenton arrived, he showed no surprise at Annie's presence. He was a tall, distinguished-looking man with grey hair. He smiled at Annie with a twinkle in his eyes.

"I don't think I've ever seen you out of uniform," he said. "You're prettier than ever."

Annie blushed. She found herself adoring the attentions of these two middle-aged doctors. She wondered how much Fenton really knew about Sikorski and herself. She wondered how soon it would be before Fenton would be after her.

Soon enough. Less than an hour later, she was sitting between them in a restaurant and Fenton had his hand on her legs. They kept ordering drinks. They kept talking about the hospital. Fenton's hand kept trying to push itself between Annie's thighs. She kept her legs closed because her crotch was sopping wet with cunt-juice. Even the tampon she had in there wasn't enough to keep her dry. She was so hot, she thought she'd come right there under the table. She finally gave in and opened her legs. He was in the midst of a story about some operation he'd performed. Without batting an eye, his hand moved up and closed over the mound of her wet cunt. She knew he could feel how dripping wet she was, but he gave no sign of it. He just pried open her cunt-lips and dug in, as if handling a bare cunt in a restaurant was something he did every day in the week.

"I think it's time to go home," Sikorski said.

Annie heaved a sigh of relief. Fenton pulled his hand from between her legs. Sikorski dropped some money on the table, and in a moment they were moving toward the exit.

They had a short discussion about whether they ought to go to Fenton's place or Sikorski's apartment. As far as Annie was concerned, they could take her to the nearest alley – as long as they fucked the shit out of her hungry cunt!

They crowded into the back of a taxi and headed for Sikorski's apartment. The liquor was having its effect. They were soon cracking jokes and giggling. Before they finished the ride, Annie had a hand in each lap, checking out the bulge of their cocks. Everything checked out fine. By the time they got to Sikorski's place, both men had roaring hard-ons!

Once inside the door of the apartment, neither man could keep his hands off her body. While Sikorski caressed her tight little ass, Fenton was busy playing with her tits.

In the centre of the living room, Annie wrapped her arms around Fenton's neck and drew herself up against his chest. She mashed her lips against his. She was sure he could feel the hard tips of her swollen nipples through the material of her dress. She gyrated her hips against his body. She could feel the hard lump of his cock. As she and Fenton kissed, Annie felt Sikorski's hands massaging the cheeks of her ass. As her tongue explored Fenton's mouth, Sikorski raised her dress up to her waist to expose her bare flesh.

The cool air caressed her naked ass. She broke away from Fenton and turned to Sikorski. She snuggled into his arms. She caught her breath as she felt the heavy mounds of her asscheeks being pulled apart. The tips of his fingers explored her deep asscrack. She moaned softly when he toyed with the tight ring of her asshole. Chuckling at her response, he forced his fingertip into her rubbery ass channel.

With a wry smile at the sight of the Hospital Director's finger deep in the ass of one of the nurses, Fenton crossed the large living room to a well-stocked bar against one of the walls. He listened to Annie's moans as he prepared three strong drinks. She was a tantalizing bitch. He still had the smell of her cunt on his fingers. He hadn't played with a woman's pussy in a restaurant in years!

When Fenton turned round again, he saw Annie on her knees with Sikorski's hard cock deep in her throat. Fenton walked back across the room and handed Sikorski his drink.

"Thanks," Sikorski said. He thrust his cock deeper into Annie's mouth. "She's very good at this," Sikorski said. "Be sure to give it a try."

Annie had no intention of wasting Sikorski's first load of jism down her throat. There'd be plenty of time to drink all the cum she wanted to, later. What she needed at the moment was the feel of a stiff cock slamming in and out of her cunt.

Pulling her face out from between Sikorski's legs, Annie smiled up at him, and then over at Fenton on the sofa. She saw the drinks in their hands and asked for her own. Without getting up off her knees, she leaned her head back and took a deep swallow of her drink. She could see traces of her lipstick on Sikorski's cock. She held out her hand and he helped her rise to her feet. She handed him her drink. Unzipping bet dress, she slipped it off and draped it over a chair.

Fenton whistled his admiration. He stared with glittering eyes at the dark bush of her cunt-hair framed by her garter belt and nylons.

Her tits swayed back and forth like heavy cantaloupes as she pranced across the room on her high heels. She let them have a good look at the wobble of her asscheeks, and then called out to them over her shoulder.

"I think the bedroom would be more comfortable," she said. "I hope you don't mind."

She left them there. Moments later, she stretched out on Sikorski's wide bed. She propped a pillow beneath her head and spread her legs apart. The pose wasn't exactly prim and proper, but neither was her mood – she needed hard fucking! The idea of making it with two men at the same time had her pussy quivering and her nipples tingling. Damn it, why don't they hurry! she thought.

In a moment, both Sikorski and Fenton walked into the room. Both pairs of eyes traveled up from her feet to the dark cunt-bush between her legs. Sikorski's eyes remained fixed on her hairy cunt. Fenton's gaze continued up across her flat stomach to the mounds of her cherry-tippled tits.

"Lovely," Fenton said.

Annie squirmed beneath the hot stares of the two men. She was thrilled at the way their eyes devoured every inch of her body. Her lips pulled back in a wanton smile. She slowly rotated her ass on the mattress. She raised her legs up in the air. They gazed transfixed at her sopping cunt. She reached down between her raised legs, smiled lewdly, and parted the folds of her pussy with her fingertips. Beads of cuntjuice glistened on her pubic hair.

"Jesus, what a cunt!" Fenton hissed.

Her fingers probing the moist heat of her pussy-gash, she watched them strip off their clothes. They climbed on the bed on either side of her body. Looking down, she watched her fingers pumping in and out of her cunt. Sikorski's hand moved to the insides of her thighs. Fenton's fingers captured her right nipple. She raised her ass up off the bed as he twisted and pulled at her tit. The burning lust in his eyes sent a shiver racing through her belly. Fenton dug his fingers into the meat of her tit and raised it up to his lips. He began sucking and slurping at her long, dark nipple. Annie could feel the sharp edges of his teeth. Then Sikorski's hand was between her thighs, joining her own on the mound of her cunt. Her head rocked from side to side as she felt his fingers seeking out the erect tip of her throbbing clit.

With a short grunt, Sikorski climbed between her thighs and lowered his face to the steaming heat of her cunt. She moaned at the first touch of his tongue whipping her clit back and forth. He sucked and slurped at her cunt like a hungry puppy. Then, he pulled his face out from between her legs and climbed up to his knees. He licked the excess cunt-juice from his mouth. He positioned the head of his throbbing cock between her dripping cunt-lips. Annie raised up her ass and pressed her cunt against the fat knob of his cock. With a sharp thrust of his hips, Sikorski rammed his swollen fuck-meat deep into the channel of her pussy gash. Annie vented soft moan as his cock began pumping in and out of her ravenous cunt.

Wrapping her legs around Sikorski's waist, Annie forced him to roll over. Resting on his side, he continued fucking her with a steady rhythm. Annie reached behind her. Her fingers slipped into the crack of her ass. She pulled her asscheeks apart and looked over her shoulder. She smiled when she saw Fenton's gaze centred on her puckered asshole.

There was no need for either of them to say anything. Annie was offering her sweet little asshole – and Fenton was not about to refuse! Shifting his body forward, he pressed the tip of his cock into the deep crack of her ass.

Annie bit her lip as Fenton's cock-head pressed against the tight ring of her asshole. She held her asscheeks apart for him. She groaned as his cock-head suddenly snapped in. He lurched forward to drive his cock into the clutching grip of her asshole.

"Oh, Christ!" she hissed. "Fuck me!"

She tightened her ass-muscles on his cock. She had both men now, one cock in her cunt and the other reaming out her ass. She felt as through her body was stuffed with cock-meat right up to her throat! She felt skewered, gloriously impaled like a sacrificial animal.

As Fenton felt her muscles tightening around hit cock-shaft, massaging the throbbing meat of his cock, he fought to hold back his climax.

Sikorski could feel the constriction of her cunt caused by Fenton's cock stretching her ass. He groaned and grunted in a delirium, holding on to her tits as if they were life preservers offered to a drowning man.

Her crotch aflame from the fucking of her two holes, Annie rocked back and forth from one slab of fuck-meat to the other. She slammed her body between the two thrusting cocks. She soon had both men convulsing past the point of no return, their swollen cocks spurting jet after jet if hot jism into her fuckhole and asshole. Her eyes rolled back and she cried out her ecstasy.

Later, when she recovered her senses, she sat up and smiled at the two men lying there limp and exhausted. She squirmed out from between their bodies. She could feel sticky, thick jism running down the insides other thighs. She climbed to her knees, moved her legs apart, and held her hands at her waist. When the two men opened their eyes, they found themselves confronted by her jism-drenched crotch.

Sikorski was the first to move his face forward

and close his mouth over the cunt which he had just ravaged. He sucked and slurped at the mixture of his own jism and Annie's cunt-juice.

His eyes feverish as he watched his colleague grunting at the trough of the nurse's cunt, Fenton suddenly moved behind Annie and pressed his face between the cheeks of her ass.

Annie cupped her hands under her tits and moaned. She had the Hospital Director sucking jism out of her cunt-hole and the Chief Surgeon sucking jism out of her asshole. Her eyes glittering, she placed a hand on each head and urged them on.

"Suck me out!" she hissed. "Get it all out!"

Fenton mewled in response and pushed his long, wet tongue into the depths of her asshole. Annie groaned and tightened her ass-muscles. His tongue felt delicious. Using both hands, she pulled her asscheeks open to give him more room.

Sikorski moved his mouth up to her clit and closed his lips over it.

Grunting at the luscious sensation of the two men slobbering at the dripping fountain of her crotch, Annie released her asscheeks to slap against Fenton's face, and moved her hands to her tits. She raised up her naked, sweaty tits. Bending her head forward, she wrapped her lips round a long, brown nipple. She sucked and chewed on her swollen teat. Pulling it out of her mouth, she moved her lips to the other nipple and gave it the sate treatment.

Fenton wanted a chance to suck her cunt. Sikorski moved away and the surgeon crouched down between her legs and put his mouth on her pussy. He used his hands to lift her asscheeks. He slid his tongue deep in her cunthole, and at the same time he pushed a finger into the ring of her stretched, fucked-out asshole. Sikorski sat beside her, playing with her tits and sucking her nipples.

Annie had the feeling she was in paradise. After the marvellous two-way fuck and suck, Tim Fenton was now paying homage to her drooling, dripping cunt – and obviously enjoying every moment of it. She shivered at the memory of the way his tongue had thoroughly washed out her asshole. He now held up her ass and flicked his tongue against the inner walls of her cunt. He seemed to love drinking the cunt-juice that continued to pour out of her pussy.

She started coming again – a slow, shattering orgasm that seemed to last forever. When it was finally over, she no longer knew if she was alive or dead. She glanced at the two long, limp cocks and the ball-sacs hanging below them. Extending her hands, she jiggled their balls on her palms and giggled softly.

"I think the tanks are empty," she crooned. "At least for a while!"

CHAPTER NINE

The first time Jake Herriot put his hand on Head Nurse Hudson's ass, he knew she thought he was crazy.

"Don't do that," she said.

But the important thing was, Jake surmised, that she didn't move away. Connie Hudson might get her kicks screwing around with other women, but Jake had an idea she'd enjoy some variety – in the form of a hard cock! At least that was the opinion he and Annie had come to when they'd wracked their brains over Annie's problem. Getting Hudson into line by fucking her seemed the only way out. Now that things were underway, Jake found that he didn't mind at all – Nurse Hudson's fat, meaty ass had a great feel to it. As far as Jake was concerned, the feel of a woman's ass always told him more than anything else about what she'd be like in bed. A woman with a big, strong ass was usually something to reckon with on a mattress. Head Nurse Hudson's ass was very big and very strong.

He pressed his open hand more firmly against her ass. He could feel the deep crack between her asscheeks through her uniform. He moved his middle finger lightly along the groove. She stiffened. Then a moment later, she pressed back against his hand.

"I said stop that," she said. "That's not allowed, Doctor. And you know it!"

She had a grim look on her face. But when his finger pressed into the crack of her ass, the look softened and a flush came to her cheeks.

"What do you want?" she said.

"Let's go down to your office and I'll show you."

"I'm too old for you."

Jake chuckled. "Come on," he said. "Let's go."

She went. Ten minutes later they were in her office with the door locked. She sat on the sofa with her legs spread out at a slight angle. He ogled her big tits and curvy legs, and smiled.

"I bet you're dynamite between the sheets," he said.

She smiled coquettishly. She unpinned her nurse's cap, and fluffed her hair.

"I've never had any complaints," she said.

He sat down on the rug in front of the sofa. He reached out and placed his hand on the inside of her dimpled knee. "I'm not surprised," he said. He slid his hand up a few inches along her nylon-covered thigh.

She moved her legs farther apart from where he was sitting, he could see a patch of white panties and a few wisps of dark cunthair. She sighed and wiggled as his hand wandered up along her thigh to the edge of her white stocking. His wrist pushed up the hem of her uniform – to completely expose her thighs above her white nylons, the straps of her garter belt, and the crotch of her white panties. The intimate aroma of her meaty cunt filled his nostrils. He could feel his cock stirring in his pants.

Her pussy was damp to his touch as he playfully jiggled it beneath her panties. He could see the outline of her rich patch of cunt hair.

"You look ready," he said.

Sighing, she turned up a thin smile. "You'll have to suck it to find out," she said. "Do you suck pussy, Doctor Herriot?"

Jake grinned. Nurse Hudson pushed her pelvis forward to give him better access to her cunt. He slipped a finger beneath the elastic band of her panties. He tickled her cunt-bush and then moved his finger down to graze her clit. She hissed. She squirmed her hips and pushed her cunt forward. Using both hands, he slowly peeled her panties down over her thighs and legs. He pulled them off over her shoes and tossed them over his shoulder.

Her hands holding her uniform tucked up at her waist, Nurse Hudson spread her thighs wide open. Her meaty, thick-lipped cunt lay fully exposed to the young doctor. He moved his head down to her crotch and began to lick, up the insides of her thighs above the tops of her stockings. The tip of his tongue snaked trough her tangled cunt-hair and down over her moist cunt-lips. Her clit was one of the largest he'd ever seen, almost the size of his thumb! He teased her by avoiding it. He licked all around it, but never touched her quivering cunt nipple.

"Oh, yes, lick it!" she yelled. She heaved up her pelvis, pushing her steaming cunt against his mouth.

Jake chuckled. He enjoyed making them wait. Going down on a woman the first time was always a treat, particularly if the woman was older and her cunt was experienced. The anticipation drove them crazy. It heightened bit own pleasure to have a woman trembling with excitement before he fucked her.

He pushed back against tic undersides of her thighs to bring her crotch up in the air. She mewled in a high pitched voice when he ran his tongue down from the slit of her cunt to the ring of her asshole.

"Oh, Jesus, that's nasty!" she hissed. "Go ahead, you bastard, lick my asshole!"

He tickled her puckered asshole. She crooned and giggled and moaned. He finally moved his mouth back up to her clit and took her firm bud between his lips. He could feel her swollen red clit throbbing under his tongue. Lifting her tight over his shoulders, he slipped his hands beneath her ass and pulled her cunt forward to his mouth. He nuzzled her dripping cunt and then looked up at her face. His lips glistened with her cunt-juice.

"You like it?"

"Oh, God, do I ever," she said.

He rolled his tongue up and down over her large, angry-looking clit. Cunt-juice oozed out of her fuck-hole in a steady stream. Her cunt was sopping wet and churning with hot lust. Her tissues were all swelled up and her wet cunt looked definitely raunchy. He liked them like that – reeking and raunchy-looking. Grabbing a cunt-lip between each thumb and forefinger, he pulled her pussy-flaps out a good four inches and gazed into her brimming pink cunt-hole. She looked down at him and giggled.

"Like what you see, honey?"

"You're a big-cunted woman," he said.

She chuckled. "I'll just assume that's a compliment. Now, get your nose in there and team it out."

He put his mouth on her again and began sucking. He could eat a juicy cunt like this all day! He used a finger to tickle her asshole. She crooned each time his fingernail scratched her puckered ring of ass-muscle. She lay there with heavy tits bouncing around under her uniform, her legs stretched out over his shoulders, the heels of her white shoes pointing towards, the ceiling. Her hips gyrated wildly as his tongue probed and searched her dripping cunt.

"I can't take it any more!" she hissed. "What's that?"

"Fuck me!" she said. "I need a cock up there! Fuck my cunt!"

"Are you sure?"

"Of course, I'm sure, you moron! Bring out your prick!"

Jake laughed. "Jesus, Connie, I thought you

never took any cock."

"I usually don't, you bastard! I haven't in years! But you've got me so hot, I can't stand it! Fuck me! Please, fuck me!"

"Sorry, can't hear you," Jake said. He enjoyed the spectacle of Head Nurse Hudson pleading for his hard cock.

"Please!" she groaned.

He rose up slowly from her sopping cunt and stood over her. He unbuckled his belt and unzipped his fly halfway.

"What was that you wanted?"

"Your cock, you bastard!" She lunged forward and made a grab for his fly, but he backed off out of her reach. He stood there with his hands on his hips and looked down at her. Her hair was a mess. Her heaving tits strained against the fabric of her uniform. Her skirt was up over her waist. Her eyes were smoky with frustration and her meaty wet cunt dripped like a fountain.

Unzipping his fly all the way, he eased out his thick, hard cock. "Is this what you want?"

Her eyes lit up. She gazed at his heavily veined, meaty cock sticking out of his pants. A drop of pre cum glistened on his fat, pink cock-head. She lurched forward off the couch and knelt in front of him with her lips just an inch away from his bloated cock-head. Her tongue snaked out between her lips and swirled lightly over his cock-knob.

Taking hold of his cock, Jake slapped it playfully against the side of her face. "You want it bad enough to eat, Connie?"

"Please!" she said. Her fingers curled around his cock-shaft and brought his cockhead in front of her mouth again.

With a short laugh, Jake stepped back. "Not yet," he said. "Take off the uniform."

She hurriedly obeyed. A moment later, she had the uniform off and tossed away. He ogled her huge tits bulging out of her bra.

"Take that damned thing off!" he growled. "Let's have a look at your tits!"

When her bra came off, he whistled at the sight of the drooping melons of her tits. Her enormous juicy nipples made his cock throb.

When her fingers moved to ungarter her stocking, he stopped her. "Leave them on," he said. "They make you look whorish. You like looking whorish don't you, Connie?"

"Yes," she whimpered.

She lay down at his feet and looked up at him with imploring eyes. His cock-head quivered and a gob of pre-cum dropped off his prick-tip to land on her belly. Mewling with delight, she rubbed the sticky fluid into her skin.

He removed his clothes, stripping everything off until he was naked. Crouching down, he straddled her chest and eased his weight down slowly so that his cock nestled in the valley between her huge tits.

"I'm going to fuck your tits," he said.

"Oh, yes!" she crooned. "Do it! Fuck them hard!"

But he began gently. He eased his cock-meat through the deep crease between her tits. He felt the soft flesh of her chest against his hairy balls. As he humped her tits, his hands pinched her fat nipples until they were hard.

She pulled his ass against her body, but he held back. He knew what she wanted. It was in her eyes, in the way she looked at him. Cunts like this enjoyed being abused – and there were very few things that Jake enjoyed more than abusing them! He would keep her primed up tight, keep her bursting with hot passion, but he wouldn't pull the string until he was good and ready. Not until she was a frothing, mad tigress, begging him on her hands and knees for a taste of his big, red cock-meat. Then he'd give it to her – and give it to her good!

Her eyes flashed wildly as she watched his cock surging back and forth between her tits. Her mouth quivered with passion. Her flips heaved up and down under his weight. He could feel her thighs straining and flexing as she tried to bring an orgasm out of her body. He knew she wouldn't have a climax until he rammed his cock deep into her steaming cunt. Head Nurse Connie Hudson might favour pussy most of the time, but at the moment she was cock-happy. Before they were through, he'd find some way to scare the shit out of her so she'd, never bother Annie again.

"Oh, God, please!" she moaned. "Easy, baby," he said.

He found himself excited by the sight of her full, pouting mouth begging for his cock. He could feel her hot body melting under him. He could smell the ripe, exciting odour of her frothing cunt. He pressed his weight down on her chest and began to move more vigorously.

Hot cum was beginning to rise in his balls as they slapped down on her heaving tits. He was ready to give her a taste – just a taste. Taking aim, he let go and shot his load right into her face. The ropy juice splattered against her forehead, just above the eyes, and dripped down over her nose and cheeks. The sight of his cock-cream dripping down her face brought up another gob of jism from his throbbing cock.

Each time he shot off, her tongue extended out of her mouth to slurp up his thick cum. He sprayed her with cock-juice until there was nothing left in his balls. She licked up his sticky cock-cream with her pink tongue. He ran his fingers over her face. He smeared his jism over her lips and chin. She lapped up his sperm like a starved kitten.

Reaching under him, she caressed his cock as though afraid it would go soft on her before she had a chance to stuff it into her steaming cunt. Jake knew he was good for at least another load. He moved forward on her chest until his cock was within reach of her jism coated mouth.

"Fuck me!" she pleaded.

"Don't worry," he said. "There's time enough for that. Right now, you just suck on it and keep it happy."

Her mouth opened to take in his throbbing fuck-meat. She obviously knew how to use her tongue, and he wondered where she'd learned it. He'd once heard, that the best cock-suckers were lesbians. He had no idea whether it was true, but Connie Hudson certainly seemed to know what she was doing. He felt another load of cock-cream beginning to build up inside his balls. He moved his hand behind him and massaged her meaty cunt. She mewled and sucked his cock more vigorously.

"You're a good cock-sucker," he said.

He rocked his hips back and forth to the rhythm of her sucking. His cock made a delicious slurping sound as it pumped in and out of her wet mouth. Her hand tickled his hairy balls. She was an expert. She kept her lips curled over her teeth to avoid scraping him. She was able to take his cock-head to the back of her throat without gagging.

"Me you ready for another load, Connie?" She nodded her head up and down, answering with her eyes.

He sneered. "You like the taste of hot jism, don't you? I bet you can drink quarts of it, you cunt."

She squeezed his cock with her lips. Her hand slid up from his balls and stroked his wet cock-shaft each time it pulled out of her clinging mouth. He could see the anticipation in her eyes – she wanted a fresh load of sperm pouring down her throat!

"You're ready now, aren't you, baby?" he said. He grabbed a handful of her hair and pulled it back and forth to make her speed up the rhythm of her sucking. He was hurting her, but he knew she loved it. As the pain and pleasure clouded her eyes, he thrust his throbbing cock deep down her throat and came.

Spurt after spurt of hot jism streamed into the cavern of her eager mouth. He kept his cock moving until he'd flooded her, until she panted and gagged for breath. Then, when she seemed about to choke on his cum, he withdrew his rampant cock out of her dripping mouth.

He smiled down at her. "Good stuff, isn't it?"

She forced a wintry smile in return and wiped her drooling mouth with the back of her hand. He rose up and left her there. His cock was now half-hard and dangling. He knew that now she would do anything for him, or rather, his hard cock.

"Get up on your hands and knees," he said. "Crawl around for me."

She began crawling around the office on her hands and knees. Her heavy tits hung down to graze the carpet with her swollen nipples. Her fleshy, pale ass, looked enormous, but not at all unattractive. Where the curve of her buttocks met her strong thighs, he could see a mop of dark cunt-hair that adorned the protruding bulge of her labial split.

He pumped his cock until he had it good and hard again. Crouching down behind her, he rammed his cock into her dripping cunt with a single smooth stroke.

"Oh, Christ!" she groaned. "Fuck me! Fuck my brains out!"

He spread her asscheeks and pushed in until he had his balls slapping against her thighs. She squirmed her cunt on his hard, thick cockmeat and moaned. When he suddenly pulled his cock out, she weaved her hips in a panic.

"Oh, Jesus!" she cried. "Put it back!"

Jake chuckled. He pushed his middle finger and index finger into her cunt-hole and his thumb in her asshole. He stiffened his fingers and began churning her two holes with a rapid rhythm. A deep, animal-like grunt rumbled out of her throat and she wagged her hips to urge him on.

"Fuck me!" she moaned. "Give it to me!" Pulling his fingers out, he positioned his cock-head on the ring of her asshole and rammed his meat up her ass.

She screamed. She wailed. She began yelping like a wounded dog. He leaned forward over her back and filled his hands with her hanging tits.

"This is for Annie," he said. "You stay away from her, you lousy dyke bitch. You hear?"

She heard. He pulled out and rammed his cock up her cunt. After five strokes into her cunt-hole, he rammed her ass again. He kept shifting between her two holes until she begged for mercy. He pulled his cock out before she had a chance to have an orgasm. He ripped up her uniform and tied her up. He had her trussed up on the floor with her head down and her ass in the air. He removed a light-bulb from one of the lamps and screwed the metal end into her asshole. She crouched there on the rug with a 60-watt bulb sticking out of her ass.

"Do your bit for the energy shortage," he said. "See if you can turn the light on!"

With a last chuckle, he put on his clothes and walked out.

CHAPTER TEN

One of the younger nurses discovered Head Nurse Hudson in her office. The light bulb was not lit. Unable to face the sarcasm of the hospital staff, Nurse Hudson resigned and obtained a position at a hospital in another city.

Shortly after, the handsome, urbane Director Sikorski was caught with his hand in the till. He was brought upon charges of embezzlement and ousted from his office.

Chief Surgeon Fenton had his head turned by a young lady from Milan and never came back from his European vacation.

Annie was sitting in the cafeteria one day, when Nurse Sophie Greensward sat down at her table. Sophie seemed exhausted. As usual, she winked at Annie and giggled.

"Room 312," Sophie said. "There's a kid in there with absolutely the biggest cock I've ever seen in my life."

Annie screwed up her face in an expression of disbelief. "The last time you told me that, it brought me nothing but trouble."

"It's true," Sophie said.

Annie grinned. "I thought I saw you walking bow-legged when you came in here."

Sophie blushed. "I won't deny it. Thank God, Hudson is gone. The new Head Nurse seems okay, doesn't she? Anyway, if you want seconds, he's a football player and he does have the biggest cock I've ever seen. He's got a friend in there now, but maybe you can scare the friend away."

"Eat your soup," Annie said. "You look like you need it."

Sophie giggled. "I'll arrange it," she said. "I'll tell him about you. His name is Barnaby Westland. God, what a cock! He wanted me to take on his friend, but I was really too pooped. His friend's cute, though. I wouldn't mind taking on both of them at the same time. That's awful, isn't it? I mean, we're supposed to nurse them, not fuck them. How do you feel about that? Could you take on two at the same time?"

Annie certainly could. An hour later she found herself in room 312 confronting Barnaby Westland and his friend, Billy. Billy was young and cute. He looked even younger without clothes. He had a cute face, a cute body, and a cute, average-size cock dangling over a pair of tight pink balls.

Barnaby Westland was something else. His wiry, sun-tanned body lay stretched out on the bed. His cock was enormous! Annie's mouth and throat went dry as she stared at it. It was by far the biggest cock she'd ever seen – and it wasn't even hard yet! Her nipples tingled and her cunt throbbed as she imagined what it would be like fully erect. A cock like that would reach places in her cunt that had never before been touched!

"You said you'd take your clothes off," Billy said. He was cute, but he was also tough. They were both tough. They were two studs who'd obviously played this game before.

She had a moment of hesitation. She wondered if she ought to go through with it. The quivering in her pussy won out and she quickly stripped off her clothes. When she unhooked her bra she saw Billy appraising her tits as if they were pieces of meat he was considering buying. The tough look in his eyes just didn't fit his cute face. But the look was there – in Billy's eyes and in Barnaby's. She straightened up and stood naked before them.

"Nice tits," Billy said. "Very nice." He reached out and ran a sweaty hand over her tits. He squeezed them one at a time, as if he owned them. Maybe he does, she thought. They owned her body, at least for the time she agreed to be with them. He used his thumb and forefinger to tug at her nipples until they swelled and puckered. He ran his hand down over her belly to the bush of her cunt-hair, and playfully pinched her fat cunt-lips.

Stretched out on the bed, his huge cock hanging limp on his thigh, Barnaby was looking at her with hunger in his eyes. She deliberately posed for him. She cocked her hip to accentuate the curve of her ass. She blew him a kiss when she saw the life beginning to show in his fuck-meat.

"That's a sweet-looking pussy," Barnaby grinned.

Rolling her ass seductively, she moved toward

the bed. Billy came with her, and she settled onto the bed between the two men. "God, what a cock you've got," she said to Barnaby. "You must be part horse."

"All horse," he said. "Just pure stud."

"I can believe it," Annie said.

Billy laughed softly. "It's not the size that counts, it's how you use it."

Annie smiled. "This is a good chance to prove it," she said.

As she lay on her back between them, she felt hot juices beginning to lubricate her cunt. She opened her legs to get some air on her pussy-meat. She wandered if they could smell her. She imagined her cunt-smell wafting up to their noses and turning them on. Reaching out, she took hold of Billy's cock in her right hand and Barnaby's enormous prick-shaft in her left hand. She squeezed both cocks. They were getting hard now. She loved the feel of a cock getting stiff in her hand.

Her left leg fell across Barnaby's thigh. Her right leg pressed against Billy. Her eyes fluttered closed as she squeezed the cocks she held in her hands. They were hot and hard. They seemed bursting with energy as they grew even larger in her fists. The sleeves of their outer cock-skin slipped easily up and down over their hardened inner prick-meat. She began to masturbate the two men together.

The cock in her left hand seemed large beyond belief. She let her fingers wander up and down, measuring its length.

"Jesus, what a cock!" she hissed. She moaned when she felt Billy's hand on her cunt. The moan became louder as he leaned across her body and ran his tongue over the crest of her tit. Releasing Barnaby's cock, she caught hold of his head and pulled his face down over her other tit. The heads of the two men were almost touching, as each sucked at a throbbing nipple.

Annie lifted her ass from the bed as she felt a finger spread the lips, of her cunt. She neither knew nor cared whose finger it was. She found herself unable to delay any longer the need to stuff her cunt. Barnaby lifted his head from her tit and kissed her long and hard on the mouth. Billy's cock throbbed against her leg as she rolled over. She climbed on Barnaby's body and clutched at the huge shaft of his upright cock.

"Ready, lover?"

Barnaby grinned up at her. "Ready as ever, baby!"

She knelt over him, one hand holding his huge cock, the other hand against his muscular chest for support. Billy moved over Barnaby's head. He half-sat with his back against the headrest of the bed, his hips on a line with Barnaby's shoulders – his cock rigidly erect and waiting! Annie bent forward and kissed his cock-head.

"It's a nice looking cock," she said.

She lowered her hips until her cunt made contact with the enormous head of Barnaby's fuckmeat. She bit her lips when she felt his smooth cock-knob meet the wet flaps of her pussy. A soft moan came out of her throat as her cunt lips were widely separated by his massive cock.

Her ass sank lower. Barnaby's hands reached around to covet the upper curves of her asscheeks as her cunt slowly parted around the head of his cock.

"Oh, sweet fuck!" she hissed.

She had his cock partly in her cunt, his immense cock-head spreading her cunt-mouth in a way she'd never believed possible. She was sure she'd faint before taking all of him, but her body didn't seem to care. Her pelvis automatically gyrated and pushed down onto his massive cock.

Groaning and mewling, she slowly inched her cunt down over his cock. Two inches. Five. Seven. It seemed endless! He was in there touching places where a cock had never been before.

Billy waved his cock in front of her face, demanding attention. Her breath rasped in her throat. She extended her tongue and touched the crown of his cock, licking it slowly. Then her mouth opened and her lips formed a ring around his cock-head. She began sucking him. Billy moved one hand to the back of her head and other hand down to fondle her hanging tit.

It was the great cock throbbing in her cunt that gave her a pleasure almost too exquisite to be endured. Her hips rose and fell with a slow, sensuous rhythm. She could feel the thick, fleshy cylinder of his cock stretching every muscle in her cunt. She could feel her cunt-lips drawn back and forth by the friction of his prick-meat. Her clit quivered and throbbed and felt ready to burst!

The hands on her ass were now lifting her up and down onto his huge cock. On the upstroke, her cunt was drawn up until only his fat prick-head remained within her cunt-hole. On the downstroke, her cunt was fully packed with Barnaby's pulsing cock-meat. She could feel her own warm pussy-juices flowing from the lips of her cunt-gash to wet the insides of her thighs. Each tit was in the grasp of a strong, knowing hand.

"Suck it, baby!" Billy hissed. "Suck that cock!"

Her lips bobbed up and down over his rigid cock-shaft. A violent trembling shook her lower body as she dropped her hips and crammed Barnaby's huge cock fully into her cunt. She stayed down, grinding the mound of her cunt against his pubic bone, massaging her clit until she brought herself to the throes of an orgasm.

Her hips churned. Her cunt milked his cock. Her lips sucked greedily at the smaller prick filling her mouth. A sudden gushing eruption, hot as lava, rose inside her, and she knew Barnaby was coming. He lifted his hips from the bed and held her suspended over his cock. His pulsing fuck-meat completely filled her. His cock-cream continued to pump until she could feel it running down from her cunt-lips to wet her thighs.

Strong hands continued squeezing her tits, her swollen nipples, the cheeks of her ass. The hand on the back of her head was now more insistent. Billy was straining to get his cock deeper into her mouth. Her jaws ached as she opened them as wide as possible to accept him.

The head of his cock slammed against the back of her throat. The hair covering his balls tickled her chin. His jism spurted deep into her mouth. She swallowed repeatedly. She felt the thick slimy cock-gravy sliding down her throat. Pulling back her head, she let the second spurt splatter against her lips and chin. She caught the third spurt in her open mouth, and it puddled on her tongue. Then she ran her tongue over the sticky shaft of his cock, and finally cleaned off his cock-head with her lips.

Barnaby remained, immobile beneath her. His cock was now soft, but it still felt huge. An aching void appeared in her cunt when he twisted his hips and pulled free. His wet cock dangled against her thigh. She rolled over and looked at him.

"First time I ever rode a real stallion," she said. She reached a hand down to stroke the sticky meat of his cock.

"Maybe when I get out of here we can make it together," be said. "I like the way you fuck."

Annie smiled. "I've got two boyfriends," she said. "I think I now know which one I'm going to marry."

Both Barnaby and Billy screwed up their faces with disapproval. Annie laughed and began putting on her clothes. When she had her uniform buttoned up, she kissed each of them on the cheek and walked out of the room.

Jake Herriot, M.D. and Annie O'Brien, R.N. were married at the end of the summer. After a simple ceremony attended by no more than a few close friends, the newlyweds drove off for a brief honeymoon at a nearby resort.

In the car, on the way to the motel, Annie sat close to Jake. He placed his hand on her nylon-covered knees. The tips of his fingers wedged between her legs, and it wasn't long before Annie opened her knees and Jake's hand slid up between her thighs.

Jake's cock hardened in his shorts as he kneaded her thigh through her stocking. He slid his hand onto her bare, warm flesh.

"That feels good," Annie crooned. She moved a hand to his lap and giggled when she felt the hardness of his cock. Her fingers deftly massaged his cock-head through his pants and shorts. She finally pulled his zipper down and brought out his fuck-meat.

"Jesus!" Jake groaned.

Annie chuckled. "Jake, honey. We haven't passed a car for miles and miles."

She reached into his shorts and pulled both of his balls out. A moment later, she had her head in his lap and her face close to the tip of his rampant cock. She took hold of his cock down near the base and tightened her fingers around it until the veins began to swell. She began licking her way upward toward his cockhead. She caught some of his clear pre-cum on her tongue as it oozed from his cock-slit. She briefly sucked his plum-shaped glans into her mouth and thoroughly wet it with her saliva.

Pulling her mouth away, she made a cooing sound and ran her tongue downward to his balls. She licked over his wrinkled ball-sac. She scooped up one of his balls between her lips and gently pressed it to the roof of her mouth as though it was a delicate, soft-shelled egg.

"Oh, shit!" Jake moaned. "I'm pulling the car over. This is too dangerous!"

He found a wide spot on the shoulder of the road and stopped the car. Annie returned her hand to the base of his cock and pulled the skin back until his velvety cock-knob was completely uncovered. She positioned his cock, then bent her head and began teasing his cockhead, stabbing and swabbing his sensitive flesh with her tongue. Jake sat there with his head leaning against the back of the seat and his throat rumbling with pleasure.

She swirled her tongue around and around the crown of his cock. She mewled at the delicate taste and aroma. Her eyes gleaming, she looked up at him and crooned.

"Feel good, honey?"

He gazed at her with his eyes half-closed and his

chest heaving. "You'll make me come," he said.

Annie giggled. "Now, now Dr. Herriot, that's nasty!"

Shaping her lips in the form of a ring, she pulled the head of his cock into her mouth. With her lips grasping him tightly, she began irritating the underside of his cock with just the barest touch of her teeth. She sucked on him like a vacuum cleaner. She began pumping her head up and down, pretending her mouth was a cunt and trying to milk him with its suction.

"Oh, Jesus!" he moaned. His hands went to the back of her head, imprisoning her mouth on his cock. "Suck it, baby!" he hissed. "Suck it hard!"

Her tongue continued to swirl over the bloated head of his cock. She teased his cock clit, massaged his flared prick-rim, and tickled the groove on the underside. Her fingers probed and fondled his heavy balls. Pulling her lips off his cock with a slurping noise, she looked up at his face and giggled.

"Come on, Dr. Herriot! Give Mrs. Herriot a mouthful!"

He groaned. He vented a long, drawn-out sigh as his cock began bucking out of control. His cock-head jerked and throbbed in her mouth as the jism shot out of him in a hot geyser. It flooded her mouth and filled the hollows of her cheeks. She began gulping and swallowing his thick, ropy sperm – her fingers squeezing his balls to drain him.

She kept his cock in her mouth until she felt it lose its size, until she was sure she had all his cum. Only then did she release him. She licked off the remnants of sperm coating his cock head. She tucked his cock back into his pants and closed his fly. Looking up at him, she swiped her tongue over her lips and grinned at him.

"Yummy," she said.

Jake grinned. "Shit, honey, you're too much!"

She moved back on the seat. Her hands went to her tits and she cupped and squeezed them through the material of her blouse. She spread her legs apart and pushed her skirt back to uncover her thighs. Bunching her skirt at her hips, she raised up her ass and pulled down her panties. She laughed when Jake whistled.

"You like what you see?"

"The lady sure has a pretty pussy," he said. He moved closer to her, took hold of her panties, and pulled them down her legs and off her ankles.

"That's better," Annie said. She spread her legs wide, exposing her thick bush of cunt hair. She moved her hands off her tits and ran them down to her belly, her fingers tangling in the curling strands of her thick black pubic bush. She took hold of her already-swollen, wrinkled cunt lips and pulled them apart to reveal the wet, pink meat of her vaginal maw.

"This is Annie's cunt," she said.

He grinned: "It certainly is!"

"Do you promise to suck it and fuck it 'til death do us part?"

"I do," Jake said, trying to keep a straight face, but failing miserably. "I certainly do!"

"Then don't waste any precious time, Dr. Herriot," Annie said and, slipping a hand behind his neck, she pulled her husband's face down to her to the soft, inviting vee of her hungry, aching cunt.

PART TWO

CHAPTER ONE

This was the first time twenty-six-year-old Jeanette Townsend (née O'Brien) had cheated on her husband and she was overwhelmed with fear and excitement.

Harry Baker was inside the door. He had his arms around her, and their mouths were plastered together in a deep kiss.

She could feel the bulge of his cock pressing against her belly. Harry's hands were on her ass, and she shivered with pleasure at the way his fingers clutched the full flesh of her ass-cheeks.

Unable to help herself, she squirmed her hips to massage her belly against the stiffness of his cock. When they finally broke apart, she gasped, "Oh, Harry, I'm frightened!"

He was the husband of one of her friends. She had never dreamed that she and Harry would ever get together like this, but then one night at a party he made a pass and she found herself accepting his offer.

At first she had been sorry, but then she'd thought it over and realized how dull her life was. She needed some excitement. When Harry called, instead of telling him it had all been a mistake, she asked him if he could get away during the day and invited him to the house.

"There's nothing to be scared of," Harry chuckled. "People do this all the time!"

He squeezed her ass again and then moved his hands up to her tits. Jeanette closed her eyes and savoured the feeling of his hands caressing her braless breasts through the thin material of her blouse.

"I've only got an hour," Harry said. "Let's go

somewhere where there's a bed before things get rushed."

His fingers toyed with one of her nipples, rolling the stiffening nub back and forth.

Jeanette had no idea what room they should use. She hadn't thought about that at all. Now she decided she couldn't possibly take Harry into the bedroom. She just couldn't cheat on Warren in the same bed they slept in.

Taking Harry's hand, she led him into the living room. The sofa would have to do. Harry seemed to understand. He smiled at her.

"It's your choice, baby. This place is as good as any, maybe even better."

Her heart pounded as she watched him remove his tie and shirt. How strange it was to have a man other than her husband undressing in the living room!

When Harry had his shoes and socks and pants stripped away, she could see his hard cock jutting like a stiff poker under his jockey shorts. She trembled with anticipation.

Then the shorts came down and his long thick cock and large hairy balls were totally exposed. Jeanette shivered. His cock was big. It looked big and ready and very capable. Faced with his burgeoning male-flesh, she was suddenly no longer frightened by the idea of adultery, no, the act was more thrilling than she would ever have guessed.

Her husband seemed to have very little interest in her. She was a woman. She needed a man's cock. She needed the look and feel of a hard cock to tell her she was wanted. She needed a man making love to her. She wanted to be penetrated because a man lusted after her, admired her, desired her. Not just because he might want to get his rocks off before he turned over and went to sleep.

She could feel the wetness in her pussy. Her cunt was now a juice-drenched swamp begging to be stuffed with hard, male flesh.

In a daze, she went down on her knees in front of Harry and wrapped her hands around his throbbing cock. Opening her mouth, she closed her lips over his bloated cock-head, swirled her tongue over the velvety, spongy knob, and then released him and rose to her feet again.

"Nice!" Harry said. "Come on, baby, get undressed. Let me see your tits!"

He stood there naked, his hard cock swaying, as she peeled off her clothes.

"Christ, what jugs!" he said. "You've really got 'em!"

Jeanette blushed because he was looking at her with such obvious, lustful appreciation. She blushed because of his crude language. And she blushed because she seemed unable to resist a hitherto hidden exhibitionist streak in her, causing her to stand in front of Harry, showing off her breasts and pinching and squeezing their heavy, thick nipples with her fingers. His wife's tits were just as large as hers. She wondered what kind of a marriage they had. She wondered if Julia was aware that Harry played around like this.

As soon as she finished undressing, Harry grabbed her breasts. With both hands, he squeezed and fondled the heavy globes and then lowered his face to briefly suck on her nipples.

Her tits had always been very sensitive, and the feel of his mouth on them made her quiver.

When he finally pulled his lips away, her nipples were swollen and glistening with his saliva.

"Gorgeous!" he said. "What kind of fucking do you like?"

Jeanette blushed. Inwardly, she winced at his crude language, but at the same time as being repelled by it, she found it strangely exciting. "I don't know. I guess I'm not very experienced."

"Christ, you've been married five years," Harry said. "Since we're not using a bed, how about a little doggy fuck? Just bend over, show me that pretty ass and I'll fuck you like a dog fucks his bitch."

His lewd language excited her. He showed her how to kneel on one of the easy chairs with her elbows resting on the back. When he moved behind her, she realized how vulnerable she was. Her cunt and ass were completely exposed to him.

She trembled with anticipation. She closed her eyes and gave a low, quavering moan when she felt the hot head of his cock rubbing between her cunt-lips. A moment later his fuck-pole pushed into her cunt-channel with a long smooth stroke.

"Oh Lord!" she gasped.

Harry put his hands on her hips, splayed his fingers out over her soft flesh, and began a slow, determined fuck. It wasn't long before the thrusting of his cock in and out of her cunt from the back like that had her mind reeling and her body vibrating.

"Oh my! How wonderful that feels!" she crooned.

The pace of his stroking increased, his thrusts became harder, and soon he was grunting and crying out as he began shooting his load. The feel of his rampant cock pile-driving in and out of her cunt overwhelmed her senses and quickly brought her to an orgasm.

She wailed and whimpered, moaning with pleasure at his attack from the rear, and finally convulsing in the throes of a shuddering climax.

Harry left her draped over the back of the armchair in a state of confused, post-orgasmic bliss. "Got to run, baby," he said.

She heard him dressing. He kissed her on the cheek and left the room. When she heard the front door close, she moaned and slumped down.

After dinner with Warren that evening, Jeanette fixed herself a stiff martini and thought how strange it was to go through the routine of another dull evening with her husband after she had cheated on him that very same day.

The hurried rear-entry fuck at noon had left her quivering for hours. She was still not over it.

Seated beside Warren on the sofa now. She began experiencing the first pangs of guilt and remorse. Warren, after all, was her husband. Their marriage was dull, but they had known each other since childhood and she couldn't imagine living without him. Oh, God, what a mess! She thought.

She still felt the aftermath of Harry's fucking, and this made it easy for her to think of relieving her guilt. She decided to get Warren interested in getting to bed early. They hadn't fucked in more than a week, and it would be hard for him to refuse.

Leaving, him, she peeled off her clothes in the bedroom and put on a filmy negligee she sometimes wore when she wanted to deliberately entice him. There was never any guarantee that it would work, but Warren usually got the message that she wanted some attention.

When she returned to the living room with her body scarcely concealed by the transparent negligee, Warren looked at her and smiled.

"Guess you're looking for some loving," he said. "It's time to get to bed anyway. I'll be in right after the news."

Well, it's hardly an erotic response, Jeanette thought mournfully as she returned to the bedroom, and certainly not a romantic one, but it was better than nothing.

Twenty minutes later Warren was on top of her, slowly pumping away in the midst of one of those dull missionary fucks that had never given Jeanette an orgasm. At least he lasts, she thought. He was always careful about coming too soon.

He stroked his cock in and out slowly, but with no imagination at all and he never did anything else. In five years of marriage, Warren had gone down on her twice – the first time during their honeymoon, and the second time when she'd asked him a year later. God, how bored I am! She thought.

She managed to manoeuvre hers body enough to get some stimulation of her clit, but it was hardly enough to bring her off.

Running her hands up and down his back, she finally moved them down to clutch his thrusting ass. As usual, this made Warren speed up his pumping, and it wasn't long before he was at the point of no return.

He grunted and groaned as he dumped his load into the channel of her cunt. Jeanette squirmed her hips and moaned as she faked a come. She'd been faking it for so long, it was almost automatic now. It was a way to avoid being asked and then having to say no.

Warren rolled over on the bed and was soon fast asleep. Jeanette slipped away to the bathroom to clean up. She looked at herself in the mirror. It wasn't surprising she turned heads and attracted married men. She was a sexy broad, no doubt about it. Her figure was curvaceous without being overly so. Her shoulder-length chestnut hair was thick and glossy and naturally wavy. Her pink-capped breasts were large and beautifully formed, seemingly defying gravity, as there was no sag to them whatsoever. Below them and her ribcage, a smooth, curving stomach, perfectly punctuated by a deep navel, led to a fine bush of dense pubic hair, which almost completely hid the pouting outer lips of her cunt.

She fingered her pussy, thinking about Harry Baker, and her clit stiffened and was soon quivering and demanding attention.

I might as well finish it, she thought. There was no way she'd be able to get to sleep without another come. Warren's fucking had only served as a mere hors d'oeuvre, wetting her appetite for something far more substantial.

She began strumming her clitoris, one leg raised up on the toilet bowl to expose her crotch. At intervals she dipped two fingers into her cunt-channel and scooped out some more juice to lubricate the tender little pink bean.

It felt good. Playing with herself always felt good. Maybe I'm a just a nymphomaniac like my sister Annie always implied, she thought. She seemed to be thinking about sex all the time these, days. Sucking and fucking were constantly on her mind.

She continually found herself looking at people and wondering what they looked like without clothes and how they fucked. She thought once again of her lovely encounter with Harry Baker. Oh, God, how I love to come!

It seemed unreal that Harry had actually been in the house that day, that he had taken her from behind, taking her like an animal and making her love every minute of it. She wondered how soon it would be before she and Harry would get together again. She could hardly wait.

Bunching up three fingers of her right hand, she squeezed them inside herself and began reaming out her vagina with her fingers serving as a cock. It felt wonderful! The stretching of her cunt-mouth was delicious.

She was able to keep her thumb on her clit as her fingers pumped in and out of her juice-drenched hole.

Turning her body a bit, she glanced at herself in the bathroom mirror. I simply look like a slut, she thought. She had one leg raised up, one hand holding her ripe tit, and the other hand pumping furiously in and out of her dripping cunt.

Damn Warren! How miserable it was to be saddled with a dull husband! She was a passionate woman with a ripe cunt and she needed sex. Harry was a lusty man who liked to fuck and she just knew there were all sorts of things they could do together. She envied her sister Annie's freewheeling nurse's lifestyle. Dating good-looking doctors and interns. Occasionally she would write about her latest conquest, but what could Jeanette offer in return? She was reluctant to admit her married sex life was a failure and a fraud.

Julia had more than once hinted that she and Harry were very adventurous in bed. Jeanette had never liked Julia that much, and she felt no guilt at all about having an affair with Harry. Why should she? The way people talked these days, everyone was sleeping with everyone else anyway. She guessed this wasn't the only time that Harry had strayed.

Once again she thought of his hard, randy cock, of the way he had mounted her from behind and fucked her so expertly. She remembered with a shiver how his heavy balls had slapped against her thighs at the end of each stroke.

She remembered the smooth thrusting of his cock in and out of her wet cunt-channel as his hands clutched her firm hips. The fucking at noon had been brief, but so far it had been the best fucking she'd received in five years of marriage.

"Oh, God, I'm coming!" she moaned to herself, wishing it would last forever.

She pumped her fingers in frenzy as she brought herself off.

CHAPTER TWO

The next morning after Warren left for work, Jeanette telephoned Harry at his office.

"Can't make it today," Harry said, "And maybe you'd better not telephone me here. Let me call you. We don't want any trouble, do we?"

She was angry. She realized she was learning the first lesson in having an affair – don't depend on anything.

Harry was right about calling him at the office,

of course. It was much too dangerous. Julia could make her life miserable if she found out about it.

I'm as horny as a bitch in heat, she thought. She remembered reading about women like that and thinking how unfortunate they were. Well now she was one of them. She had to do something about it, but the question was what.

The answer came less than an hour later. The front doorbell rang. When she answered it, she found a teenage boy standing on the doorstep.

"I'll mow your lawn if you like, ma'am," he said with a shy smile.

Jeanette looked him up and down. Warren had cut the grass just a few days ago, but she didn't care. She had the feeling the boy had been sent down from heaven to make her day.

"How much?" she asked.

"Three dollars an hour."

She put him to work. While he was outside pushing the lawnmower, she stripped off her clothes and put on a bikini. She fixed her face, fluffed her hair, and walked out to the backyard carrying a can of beer and a cigarette.

She stretched out in the shade on a chaise lounge and waited for the boy to push the lawnmower around to the back of the house.

When he was there at last, she smiled at him and told him he needed a rest.

"How about a Coke?" she said. "You don't have to worry about the time. It's on me."

He thanked her. She laughed to herself at the way his eyes raked up and down her body. The skimpy bikini showed a great deal of tits and ass. When she brought out the Coke, she found him sitting in the sun with his shirt off.

"You've got a nice body," she said.

He gave her a shy smile. "I play football."

"How interesting," Jeanette said. "Do you know anything about faucets?"

"Faucets?"

"The kitchen faucet is leaking. Maybe you can take a look at it."

He shrugged. She let him into the house and showed him the faucet in the kitchen. She stood beside him while he tinkered with it. There was really nothing wrong with the faucet, and she soon distracted him by offering him another Coke.

She opened a can of beer and they sat together in the kitchen drinking. His eyes feasted on the swell of her tits barely covered by the bikini top. Being indoors with him and half undressed was somehow more exciting than being outside.

"You're staring at my breasts," she said.

He blushed.

"I don't mind," she smiled. "Would you like to see them?"

Without waiting for an answer, amazed by her own brazen behaviour, she pulled the top of her bikini down to expose the heavy melons of her dark-nippled tits.

"Jesus!" the boy muttered.

"Come over here," she said.

His expression uncertain, he walked over to where she was sitting and stood in front of her. His eyes were fixed hungrily on her tits.

Grabbing his hands, she placed them over her full globes and held them there. "Go on," she said. "I don't mind. Touch them."

His eyes wide, his mouth slack, he moved his hands tentatively over her swollen tits. Then he became bolder, his fingers squeezing and probing her firm flesh.

She fluttered her fingertips over the bulge of his cock, tracing the outline of his cock-shaft and the shape of his cock-head. His cock felt as hard as a rock under his jeans. He groaned softly at the touch of her fingers.

He kept his hands on her tits as she unbuckled his belt and pulled down his zipper. She peeled his jeans down to his ankles. Her hand moved quickly over the length of his rigid cock until she was cupping his balls.

She smiled at the way his jockey shorts were stretched out of shape by his up-thrust turgid penis.

His body tensed as she fingered his balls. He watched her warily, like a trapped animal. Her hand came up now and she took hold of his thick cock still imprisoned in his jockey shorts.

Breathing hard, her heart pounding, her fingers moved slowly up the length of his cock and down again. Her hand pressed against the throbbing tip of his cock while her fingers stretched downward to feel the length.

She squeezed. It was like a rock, a cloth-covered rock. Her pussy quivered. She pinched and probed his bloated cock-head. He groaned when she finally pulled his shorts down.

The hot skin of his cock-head grazed her hand as his hard cock sprang out in front of her eyes. It was big and red and angry looking. His cock-shaft was blue-veined and very thick.

Closing her fingers around his cock-shaft, she moved the skin up and down. His piss-hole opened wide and a drop of clear fluid brimmed in the slit.

He still had his hands on her tits. His fingers felt

like hot branding irons. He made circular motions on each tit, paused at her cleavage, then slid up only to return eagerly to her nipples.

Stripping his cock-skin back to completely expose his cock-head, she opened her mouth and engulfed his dripping knob.

"Ohhh Jeez!" he moaned.

She had little chance to give him a real blow job. She stroked the ring of her lips up and down the shaft of his cock, and then suddenly he cried out and started shooting spurt after spurt of thick hot jism into her open mouth.

She had to swallow to keep from choking. Gulping and sucking, she finally drained his load and pulled her mouth off his cock to smile up at him. She wiped a blob of white sperm off her downy upper lip with her index finger and popped it in her mouth.

"Was that nice?" she asked.

"Oh, shit, I'm sorry!" he groaned.

"Don't be," she smiled. "I liked it. I'm sure you can get hard again. Let's go into the bedroom and get your clothes off."

He pulled up his jeans and she led him into the bedroom. When they had their clothes off, she laughed at the eagerness in his eyes. The boy was certainly different than her husband!

He also had none of Harry's brusqueness. He was hot for her. The way his eyes feasted on her cunt-bush made her feel as though she had a great treasure down there between her legs. She loved it!

Stretching out on the bed on her back, she pulled her knees to her chest and opened her thighs wide.

"I'd like you to lick my... my pussy," she said.

"Have you ever done that to a girl?"

He nodded. He climbed onto the bed and went down on her. She soon found that he wasn't as innocent as he looked. He had sucked pussy before. He knew the different between her cunt-hole and her clit. He knew enough not to neglect either of them.

"Do it!" she hissed. "Oh, God, yes, lick my pussy!"

His tongue swabbed up and down between her thick, swollen cunt-lips. She gasped at the lovely feel of his hot breath on the quivering meat of her pussy.

"Kiss it lover! Suck my pussy! Lick it!"

The increasingly lewd words came pouring out of her mouth as she squirmed her ass, grinding her cunt against his face.

"Good!" she sighed. "Stick your tongue in my c-c- cunt hole!"

Obediently, he tongue-fucked her dripping vulva, penetrating deep into her vaginal cavity. Then he moved his tongue up to massage her quivering clit. Her ass flew off the bed as she came. Bucking her hips, gurgling with pleasure, she climaxed on the boy's face.

"That was beautiful!" she groaned.

Her voice took on a stern note.

"Now... fuck me!"

When he climbed between her legs, she ran her hand over his cock and balls and positioned his spongy cock-head at the mouth of her cunt-hole. Grunting with impatience, he lurched forward and buried his cock inside the dripping channel of her cunt.

He was young and strong. He pumped in and out in frenzy and she held the cheeks of his ass as he pistonned his cock into her clutching hole. When she sensed his orgasm approaching, she rocked back and forth and cried out.

"Oh god yes! Fuck me! Shoot it! Shoot all your spunk inside me!"

She came as the first jets of his jism gushed into her eager cunt. He continued pumping until she had the last of his load, and then he rolled over on the bed.

He groaned when she moved her head down to his crotch and began lapping at his cock. She licked the juice off his limp prick and then sucked it into her warm mouth.

Squeezing his balls, she sucked on him until he began to harden again. She laughed to herself at how easy it was to get a boy his age up again.

"Have you ever done it... doggy-style?" she asked.

Without waiting for an answer, she knelt on the edge of the bed. He moved round to stand behind her. She was drunk on her lust. She wiggled her ass in his face, enticing him to fuck her.

"Stick it in!" she crooned.

A moment later his hard cock drove into her wet cunt like a battering ram. Her head down on the mattress, her eyes closed, her jaw hung loose as the boy began a rapid jackhammer fuck that rattled her bones.

She started coming almost immediately. There seemed no end to it. She had one orgasm after the other, and she had the feeling she could keep on going forever.

When he finally spurted his load, she slumped over on her side exhausted and dozed off.

A voice awakened her. "What's that?" she said.

She realized that the boy was still there. He was dressed now.

Standing beside the bed, he looked down at her. "Can I have my money, lady?"

"Money? What money?"

"For mowing the lawn, lady. Can I have my money? I've got to go."

Jeanette laughed and said, "Of course, honey. What's your name?"

"Arnold. My friends call me Arnie, though."

"Well, here you go, Arnie. A little something extra for you."

The boy's eyes widened when he saw she'd given him a twenty dollar bill and his face cracked into a broad grin. "Gee, whiz, Missus, can I get to mow your lawn next week?"

Jeanette laughed. "We'll see about that," she said, and with a good-natured shove she gently shooed him out the door. "But why don't you come by same time next week and see how tall the grass is?"

Arnie laughed and said, "I'll be there. Just try and stop me, lady"

After the boy left, Jeanette got into the shower and washed herself clean. She blushed as she remembered how wild she had been. Was that wild woman really her? She'd practically raped that poor kid! Then she giggled. He was far from a kid. He'd given her a better fuck than her husband ever had!

Her pussy still tingled from the memory of it.

Returning to the bedroom, she decided that one last come would really settle her down for the day. It made no sense to deny herself now. After a rousing fuck like that, she wanted to be certain she'd have some peace for a while.

Her thighs quivered with anticipation. Her pussy was wet again. Her cunt these days seemed to be constantly more wet than dry! By the time she lay down on the bed, she could feel the juice dripping down the insides of her thighs.

Opening her legs, she wiped her thighs off with the top sheet and spread the lips of her pussy. Lifting a hand to her shoulder, she slowly caressed her smooth flesh. Then she trailed her fingers down over her boobs, and scraped her fingernails across each nipple.

Her hands roamed over her body as she touched herself in her sensitive places, God, she was hot! She felt she could almost come just from touching her skin.

Rolling over, she pressed her cunt into the bed, forcing her cunt-lips open, squashing the meat of her pussy down against the mattress. She pumped her hips, grinding her crotch against the sheet.

Slipping both hands under her belly, she shoved her fingers into her cunt and held them there, not moving, feeling the heat and wetness of her cunt-flesh, and then gradually humping her cunt up and down against her hands.

Her nipples were hard. Her tits felt swollen, ripe and ready. She pushed two fingers inside her cunt-hole, slowly pistoning them in and out of her dripping hole. She rolled over. On her back again, she moved her free hand to her tits and squeezed her nipples.

She was aching for it now. There was no way she could wait any longer. She shoved another finger inside her cunt-hole, stretching her cunt-mouth, screwing the three fingers in and out like a small cock.

Groaning, she humped up and down, fucking back at her hand. Without warning, she suddenly came. She thrust her head back and pumped her hips in frenzy as cunt juice oozed out all over her hand.

"Oh, fuck!" she cried aloud.

She clamped her thighs together, clenching her pussy shut, squeezing the hairy cunt-flesh around her fingers, savouring the thickness of her hand as she came again. Fuck, fuck, fuck. The words echoed in her mind, now powerful and erotic, no longer obscene or disgusting. God, what a fucking slut I am, she thought, and laughed out loud.

Pulling her fingers out from between her legs, she brought them up to her face. The smell of her own juices filled her nostrils. She stared at her sticky-slippery fingers, looking at them mesmerized, imagining they were a stiff cock.

With a soft moan, she shoved her fingers into her mouth and began sucking them. When she had all her cunt juice licked off, when her fingers were almost dry, she pulled them out and returned them to her crotch.

Now she worked directly on her clit. She slipped her free hand under her ass and gently massaged her anus. Spread-eagled on the bed, both hands massaging her crotch, she stroked and teased her cunt and ass until her hips were once more pumping up and down.

"Oh, dear God!" she moaned.

The final orgasm poured out of her cunt in a wave of hot ecstasy.

CHAPTER THREE

A few days later Julia Baker telephoned to invite Warren and Jeanette to a barbecue. Jeanette was uneasy about seeing Harry again in his house, but there was no way they could refuse the invitation.

When they arrived at the party, it was a warm afternoon, and Harry immediately took Jeanette aside and apologized for neglecting her.

"I've been busy," he said, "But I've been thinking about you."

Jeanette wondered. She'd never been any good at reading peoples' faces and Harry's face was no easier than others.

"Listen," Harry said. "In about a half-hour you go on up to the guest bathroom on the second floor and I'll meet you there."

"What for?" Jeanette said.

Harry grinned. "You'll find out."

Her pussy quivering, Jeanette waited thirty minutes and then slipped away from the party and went up to the second-floor bathroom. She spent a few minutes fixing up her face. There were other bathrooms in the house, and she hoped no one would decide to use this one.

She was getting impatient waiting for Harry, when there was a knock on the door and she heard him softly call her name. A moment later he was inside the bathroom, locking the door behind him, and grabbing her into his arms.

Shivering with excitement, she pressed herself against him. He ran his hands over the cheeks of her ass and hissed in her ear, "How's the pussy?"

"Oh, God, Harry," she moaned. "We'll get

caught in here!"

"I don't care," he said. "The minute I set eyes on you today, I wanted your ass! Just put your hand on my cock and feel what I've got for you!"

She ran her fingers over the bulge in his crotch. His cock was hard and throbbing. She could feel the heat of it through the fabric of his pants.

She was frightened at the thought that some one might come along and want to use the bathroom. Suppose they waited outside. She and Harry would have to leave together and what they'd been doing would be obvious.

Pulling up her dress, Harry pushed his hand between her legs and squeezed her cunt-lips through her pantyhose and panties.

"Christ!" he fumed. "Why in hell do women wear pantyhose? You can't get at a cunt through these things."

Jeanette giggled. She pulled the zipper down and fished inside his pants for his cock. It was so big and hard she had difficulty getting it out into the open.

His bloated cock-head was hot and dripping. She jacked his cock-skin back and forth a few times and smeared the juice leaking out of his piss-hole over his knob. He finally pulled his hand away from her cunt and made her sit down on the closed toilet seat.

"Suck on my cock awhile," he said. "Let me see those gorgeous lips on the banana."

Lapping her tongue over his cock-head and cock-shaft to get him wet, she sucked him gluttonously into her mouth.

"Oh, yeah!" he groaned. "That's good!" She bobbed her head slowly back and forth over the shaft of his cock. She'd always liked sucking cock.

It was almost as good as fucking. How sad it was that Warren was embarrassed by it! She had sucked his cock a number of times, but it always sensed to make him uncomfortable.

"You give great head!" Harry said. Holding onto her ears, he began fucking her face, pistonning his cock in and out of her wet lips. She remained motionless, her eyes closed, her attention focused on the hot slab of meat pushing in and out of her mouth.

Harry groaned a few times, but he didn't come. When he pulled his cock out of her mouth, she looked up at him. "Fuck me!" she said.

"That's the general idea," he chuckled. If Harry was surprised by the cruder, more sexually-emancipated language she was using, he refrained from comment. She wondered how they would do it. Her pussy fluttered as she realized it would be the first time she had ever fucked in a bathroom.

"Lift your dress up and bend over the sink," he said.

Her knees trembling, she did as he said. She understood what he wanted. Resting her elbows on the sink, her dress rolled up around her waist, she stuck her ass out and spread her legs.

Moving behind her, he peeled her pantyhose and panties down to her thighs. He ran his hand over her hairy cunt-lips. Her pussy was sopping wet with cunt juice. Her cunt-lips were swollen and pulsating.

He reamed two fingers in and out of her cunt-hole, and then she felt his hot cock-head pushing between her cunt-lips. A soft moan escaped her lips as he lurched forward to drill the entire length of his cock into the wet channel of her cunt.

"Beautiful," he groaned.

Raising her head, she looked at her face in the mirror. She could see him behind her. He had an intense expression on his face as he began slowly stroking his cock in and out of her sopping-wet cunt. Then she lowered her head again and rested it on her forearms. Fucking this way was delicious!

Her pantyhose made it difficult for her to spread her legs very wide, but she managed to get enough balance to be able to wiggle her ass as he fucked in and out of her cunt. Each time he drilled into her, she could feel his hairy balls slapping against her thighs.

His hands fondled and squeezed her ass-cheeks, and then she felt his fingers moving into the crack of her ass to tickle her asshole. She moaned when he rubbed some of her cunt juice over the ring of her asshole, and then a moment later she squealed when he pushed a finger inside. The double penetration of asshole and cunt-hole were exquisite.

"Have you ever had it in there?" he said.

"No," she groaned.

She had often wondered about it. The idea made her a little aprehensive, but at the same time it made her legs tremble with lust. She wondered, perversely, if Harry ever fucked Julia in the ass.

"Sweet little asshole!" he grunted. "We can't let it go to waste."

She shuddered. She was apprehensive about doing it, but at the same time she wanted it. She solved the problem by saying nothing.

Reaching over her head, Harry opened the medicine cabinet and removed a jar of Vaseline. She shivered with fear and anticipation when she felt grease up her asshole. He slipped a finger inside her and wiggled it around the tight confines of her sphincter.

In a way it seemed fitting that Harry should fuck her in the ass. She deserved it. She was no better than a nympho slut, after all. And it was something she could never imagine her husband doing.

"Please be careful," she moaned.

He laughed. "It's up to you, honey. If you relax, I'll get in there without any trouble at all."

Now she felt his hot cock-head rubbing up and down the crack of her ass. A moment later she could feel his spongy glans pressing at her puckered shit-hole.

Her fear of pain kept the muscles in her ass tightly flexed, but she somehow gradually relaxed. She groaned as she pictured his fat cock-head trying to force its way into her tight little asshole.

How strange it was to be there in Julia's bathroom bent over the sink while the party went on downstairs and Harry buggered her! She would simply die if anyone ever found out about it.

At the same time she had to admit to herself how thrilling it was. The very lewdness of the act made it terribly erotic.

The tip of his cock-head slowly squeezed into the tight ring of muscle, and then suddenly the whole knob popped in.

"Oh, Lord!" she cried.

"Easy, baby," Harry said.

His cock felt like a baseball bat driving relentlessly up her ass. He pushed the entire length of his cock into her shit-tube until his hairy balls were tickling her cunt-lips. A long wail gurgled out of her throat as he realized she had all of his cock inside her shit-hole.

"How do you like it?" he grunted.

"It hurts a little, but I can stand it."

"Relax your ass like you're gonna take a shit, and it won't hurt at all."

"Yes, you're right. It's better now," she said, blushing slightly at his crude analogy.

"Good?"

"Yes. You can do it harder if you want. Oh, yes. That's good! Oh my!"

He was pumping slowly now, his cock thrusting in and out of her stretched asshole with a steady, relentless rhythm. It wasn't long before she began coming. It was nothing like coming with a cock in her cunt or her finger on her clit. She groaned and quaked through a mind-blowing deep orgasm unlike anything she had ever experienced before.

At the end of it, when he was fucking her ass with the same ramming force familiar to her cunt, she rolled up her eyes and wailed at the enormous pleasure of it.

"Do it to me!" she said, her voice a hoarse, whispered scream. "*F-f- fuck my ass!* Give it to me *hard!*"

Harry chuckled and continued slamming his cock in and out of her twitching shit-tube. Moments later, at the peak of her orgasm, he grunted and spurted his load of hot jism deep into her bowels.

The adulterous couple kept their position for a few moments, then Harry's cock slipped out of her and she had to clench her anus to prevent any spillage. She looked away as he stood beside her at the sink and, grabbing some soap, quickly washed his dirty penis until it was quite clean. Then he dried it on a hand towel, stuffed it back into his pants, zipped up his fly and left to rejoin the party downstairs. Jeanette locked the door after him and sat down gratefully on the toilet, letting the liquid contents of her bowels splatter out with a sigh of relief. She wiped herself carefully, then flushed the toilet.

Her mind dazed and her ass tingling pleasantly, Jeanette returned to the party. Within minutes Julia Baker was at her side with a friendly smile and inquisitive eyes.

"We ought to see each other more often," Julia said.

"Why yes, Julia, we really should," Jeanette replied, a little stiffly.

"I've always admired you, you know."

"Me?"

"Yes. You always seem so... happy."

Jeanette glanced up at her. "Really? Well, life has its ups and downs." And its ins and outs, too, come to think of it, she mused.

"And you're so pretty." Julia placed a hand on her shoulder as if to emphasise her compliment.

"Well, thank you, ma'am. That's such a sweet thing to say, and flattery will get you everywhere," laughed Jeanette.

"I'll call you one of these days."

"That would be nice."

Inwardly Jeanette was alarmed that Julia was suspicious of some sort of chemistry going on between her and Harry. Perhaps Julia could even smell the faint odour of sex about her person. She was relieved when her hostess finally left her to talk to some other guests.

She laughed to herself. How crazy it was to be standing there talking to a woman when the woman's husband had just buggered her!

Her asshole was still tingling and felt somewhat

battered and abused. She was worried that it might leak any remaining vestiges of Harry's cum, too. Looking around, she found an empty chair and sat down. Harry was standing with a group of people not too far away, and when she caught his eye he winked. She blushed and prayed that Warren would come along soon to take her home. She'd had enough of Harry for one day!

Warren appeared not long after, and when she suggested it was time to leave, he readily agreed.

During the drive home, Warren seemed in good spirits. He told her there was a possibility he might change jobs and move to Harry's company. Jeanette pretended to be happy about it, but inside she just felt guilty about her affair with Harry Baker.

If Warren and Harry worked for the same company, she could expect to see more of Harry and Julia. She didn't like that at all. Sooner or later she would have to find a way to untangle herself from Harry. What she needed was a way to meet men, men who were not in any way connected to her married life. Maybe she ought to get a job.

When they arrived home, she was mildly upset when she realized that Warren wanted to fuck. Fine time! She thought. I've just had my ass reamed out and now he wants to have his marital rights.

In a way it was funny. Warren was never there when she wanted him, and now that she wanted to do nothing more than sit in a hot bath he was all hot and eager to get into her pants. Thank God it was late!

She delayed getting into bed as long as possible,

hoping he would be asleep. He was waiting for her, however, and within moments after the light was out he was on her like an octopus.

She played along with it. She knew she would get nothing out of it. As she expected, it was just another boring fuck, and all it meant was that at the end of it she had to get out of bed again and clean up before going to sleep.

Jeanette didn't see Harry for a few days, and then one morning he telephoned and suggested he pick her up for lunch.

He was interested in more than lunch, of course, and afterwards they drove to a motel near the airport. She felt safe there.

Harry was very horny and he insisted on a quick fuck to cool him down. Jeanette didn't mind.

He rode on top with her legs draped over his shoulders, pounding her cunt in a fury, and when he started coming she just managed to squeeze off a light come as he shot his load.

They relaxed and talked. She talked about her marriage. She needed to talk to someone, and Harry, after all, was the man with whom she was having an affair.

"I don't want to break up my marriage," she said.

"Who says you have to?" he replied.

"Sooner or later Warren will find out."

"Not if you're careful, baby. Anyway, how do you know Warren isn't getting a little action on the side himself?"

"I can't believe that."

"You might be surprised."

"Aren't you afraid of Julia finding out?"

"Julia and I have an arrangement, baby. She has

her games and I have mine."

"But you said I shouldn't call you at the office."

"I don't like the people in the office knowing my private business. That makes sense, doesn't it?"

"I guess."

"Julia likes you."

"Yes, I know."

"Have you ever thought about making it with a woman?"

"Certainly not! Why?"

"Just asking, baby. Just asking."

She was puzzled, but they had time for one more fuck and she was anxious to have it before they had to leave.

Moving her head down to his crotch, she began sucking on his cock to bring him up again. His long thick cock was soon ready. Fisting his cock-shaft, she pumped it up and down to get him as stiff as possible. "You're as ready as ever," she said. Harry chuckled. "It looks that way. How do you want it?"

"Fuck me in the ass again," she said. "That's what I want."

Harry laughed. "You got it, baby."

CHAPTER FOUR

A week later Warren's company sent him out of town for a few days and Jeanette suddenly found herself inexplicably lonely. Normally she was good at being on her own, self-sufficient and resourceful when it came to entertaining herself. But latterly she had been anxious and moody and craving company – almost any company, so when Julia telephoned to invite her to dinner, she eagerly accepted.

Julia was turning out to be a much nicer person than Jeanette had thought. She felt a little awkward going to Harry's house without Warren, but Warren had no reason to be angry. It was just a social visit. At least that's what Jeanette thought.

When she arrived at the house, Jeanette was surprised to find that both Harry and Julia were high – whether on booze or something else, she didn't know. At the moment they were drinking bourbon, and in order to be friendly Jeanette had to drink along with them.

They drank all through dinner, and by the end of it Jeanette realized she was as high as a kite. In a way it made the evening more pleasant. Whatever awkwardness she felt being with Harry was much easier to handle when she was feeling good like this.

They sat in the living room drinking and laughing at Harry's jokes. The stereo was going full-blast and sometimes Jeanette could hardly hear what they were saying.

Julia and Harry were sprawled out beside each other on some pillows on the floor, and it was some time before Jeanette realized they were actually feeling each other up. Even through the fog of booze clouding her mind, she was shocked – and not a little jealous. Then she told herself with a shrug that they were married and they could really do anything they wanted to do.

Once again she wondered if Julia knew she had been fucking Harry. Jeanette tried to think about it, but the booze prevented her head from working and she had to give up.

She sipped her bourbon and watched the couple on the floor. A shiver of lust went through her when she saw Julia open Harry's pants and bring out his cock. Now Jeanette was really jealous. She'd been fucked to a frazzle with that cock and it was almost an old friend.

Julia had been doing no more than playing with Harry's cock, pumping it up and down, but now she leaned over and began licking her tongue up and down his cock-shaft. Jeanette watched transfixed as Julia opened her red lips and engulfed Harry's cock-head like a hungry bird.

"Oh, Jesus!" Jeanette groaned.

This time even the booze couldn't prevent her from taking full account of what was happening. It seemed unreal that Julia was actually sucking Harry's cock in front of her eyes, but there it was!

Julia slowly bobbed her head up and down, the ring of her red lips sliding from his cock-head to his crotch and back again. Harry had a long cock and Jeanette knew exactly how it felt to have his cock-head jabbing at the back of her throat. She could picture his knob tickling Julia's tonsils each time she swooped down to push her nose into his crotch-hair. She must be 'deep-throating' him, thought Jeanette dully.

"Oh, yeah, baby!" Harry growled.

Julia was obviously an expert cocksucker, she thought, wryly.

Once again Jeanette was half-jealous, half-aroused. Why were they doing this in front of her? Then she told herself that Julia, after all, was Harry's wife.

Maybe it's a dream, Jeanette thought. It was

all very unreal. She had no will to move now. She was totally mesmerized by the scene on the floor. She had never in her life watched people fucking and although Julia was only sucking Harry's cock, it was enough to make Jeanette shiver with lust.

One part of her mind told her she ought to get up and leave, but the urge to watch them was too strong.

She was turned on, maybe more turned on than she'd been in a long time. She couldn't help moving a hand down to her crotch to rub her cunt mound and relieve a sort of itch that had started somewhere around her clitoral bud. Harry and Julia were too busy to notice. Anyway, she didn't really care if they noticed or not. Her cunt was steaming and there was no way she could sit there and watch them without doing something herself.

"Oh, shit, here it comes!" Harry grunted.

Her eyes wide, her heart pounding, Jeanette watched Harry shoot his load down Julia's throat. She could see Julia's throat muscles working as she swallowed and gulped Harry's spurting load.

Wrapping her hand around Harry's cock-shaft, Julia pumped his prick to get the last of his cream out of him. She sucked on his juice-coated prick with obvious relish. If she was aware of Jeanette, she gave no sign of it.

She gobbled on Harry's prick, seemingly quite unconcerned that Jeanette was sitting right there and watching every movement of her lips.

After she had drained Harry's cock completely, Julia pulled her mouth off his cock-head and began licking up the jism that had dripped down his cock-shaft. She licked and slurped on Harry's shrinking cock-meat, and then she finally pulled away and licked her lips to get the last drops off her mouth.

When she had finished, she turned to Jeanette and smiled.

"I hope you didn't mind that, honey. I guess we just got carried away."

Moving her hand away from her lap, Jeanette coloured slightly. She had no idea what to say. She sipped her bourbon instead. Her hands were trembling. Watching Julia sucking off Harry had been terribly thrilling. Now she was turned on, her pussy was wet to the point of soaking her panties, and the tension and need was making her body quiver.

Then she heard Harry chuckle, "Jeanette looks like she wants some action. Maybe we ought to take care of her."

Jeanette closed her eyes and trembled. She knew what was coming. She knew that tone in Harry's voice. She knew that at this point she could refuse and go home. Instead, she sat there without moving. She had no idea what they had in mind, but whatever it was she was impatient for it.

It wasn't long before Harry came to sit beside her. He put his arm around her shoulders and nuzzled her neck.

"I bet you expected nothing more than dinner tonight," he said.

Jeanette shivered when he began fondling her tits. Julia was there on the other side of the room, and Jeanette was conscious of the other woman's eyes on them.

She squirmed under Harry's hands. Her pussy quivered at the lewdness of what they were doing.

She groaned when he slid his hand under her skirt and ran his fingers between her thighs.

"Honey, she's soaking wet!" Harry laughed.

He pinched and probed her swollen cunt-lips through her panties. She could hear the squishing of her cunt juice as he fondled the meat of her dripping pussy.

"Let's get her clothes off," Julia crooned. "I'm sure she'll be more comfortable that way!"

Jeanette closed her eyes and whimpered as Harry began undressing her. She shivered under the touch of his hands on her body, and for a while she managed to forget about Julia.

When Harry had her completely stripped, he sucked on her nipples and fingered her pussy until she was on the brink of an orgasm. He teased her by pulling his hand away at the last moment to leave her hanging. She was soon pumping her crotch at his hand, urging him to give her more.

With a chuckle, he reamed out her cunt-hole with two fingers and strummed the ball of his thumb over her clit.

Moaning, she pulled her knees up to her chest and opened her crotch to him. He fucked his fingers in and out of her cunt with short strokes, never long enough to make her come, but just enough to keep her strung out like a tight wire.

"She sure looks juicy!" Julia said.

She had brought out a pink plastic vibrator from somewhere, and now she was holding it in her hands, running her, fingers over it as she watched Harry playing with Jeanette's wet pussy. Their eyes met. Jeanette blushed and shivered when she realized she was completely naked and Julia completely dressed.

There was a strange look in Julia's eyes, a look

of unbridled lust, the look of a bird of prey about to conquer a victim.

Harry was tickling Jeanette's asshole now, and she moaned with embarrassment when he pushed his finger inside her shitter. She trembled with pleasure at the feel of his fingers in her cunt-hole and asshole. He stroked both holes at the same time, slowly fucking her with his hand.

"Oh, God, do it harder!" she finally cried out. "Make me come!"

Harry laughed and refused. Pulling his fingers out of both locations, he wiped his hand on her belly and flicked at her nipples with his fingertips.

Now Julia sat down on the other side of Jeanette and leaned over to look closely at Jeanette's cunt. Jeanette still had her knees up at her chest, and when she tried to close her legs Julia laughed and pushed them open again.

"Don't be bashful, honey. It's only a pussy."

Jeanette gasped when she felt Julia's hand sliding along the underside of her thigh. Soon Julia's fingertips fluttered over Jeanette's swollen cunt-lips and then she pried them open to have a look at the pink meat of Jeanette's pussy.

Harry's hand went down to join Julia's, and Jeanette shivered with she realized she had two hands working on her cunt. A moment later Harry pushed a finger into her ass again. This time the pleasure overwhelmed any embarrassment Jeanette felt, and her head fell back as she heaved up her crotch to get more.

Julia began massaging Jeanette's clit with a deft touch. Jeanette quivered and moaned at the feel of the two hands working over the sensitive tissues of her cunt and ass.

She was completely in their power. Her legs

were pulled up and spread-wide. She offered her juice-drenched crotch to the two of them, not caring any longer about how crazy it was.

"Just relax, honey," Julia breathed in her ear. "I'm going to make you feel good!"

She switched on the vibrator and began playing it over Jeanette's cunt-lips. Jeanette moaned and trembled at the exquisite sensations flowing up from her crotch.

Julia teased her. "Would you like it inside, darling?"

"I don't care!" Jeanette wailed. "Don't tease me. I can't stand it!"

Julia laughed and continued touching her cunt-lips with the vibrator. She probed and teased and probed again.

Harry's finger continued moving in and out of Jeanette's asshole, and now he shoved in another finger. Jeanette shuddered at the way the two fingers stretched the ring of her shitter.

"Oh, God!" she cried. "What are you doing to me!"

"Relax!" Harry laughed. "You're having a ball. You can't fool me!"

"She's in heaven," Julia laughed. "If we keep this up, she'll be pissing in our hands!"

Harry's fingers moved relentlessly in and out of Jeanette's asshole. Julia deliberately avoided getting the vibrator anywhere near Jeanette's clit. The teasing drove her wild. She was no longer in control of herself. They were playing with her body as though it were a musical instrument. Each new touch of her fingers and hands brought a moan gurgling out of her throat.

She shuddered and quaked, her head thrown back, her mouth hanging open as she concentrated on the sensations they were producing.

Grabbing her wrist, Harry pulled her hand to his cock and she eagerly closed her fist around his hard cock-shaft. She pumped his cock-meat, swabbed his cock-head with her thumb, and revelled in the crazy lust overwhelming her senses.

"She's a wild one!" Julia said. "She's delicious!"

Jeanette groaned now as Julia slowly slipped the vibrator inside her cunt-hole.

"Oh yes, yes!" she moaned, "Oh, dear Lord!"

Julia laughed and slowly pumped the plastic cock in and out of Jeanette's clutching cunt. Harry moved his fingers in and out of her shit-hole to the same tempo.

The double penetration made her crazy with lust. Her crotch was on fire. The insides of her thighs were soaked with her cunt juice. She held her tits in her hands and tossed her head from side to side, pleading with them to finish her off.

"I can't stand it!" she begged. "Make me come!"

Julia smiled as she moved the vibrator to Jeanette's clit.

"Oh, fuck!" Jeanette screamed, now oblivious of any social restraints that might have prevented her reciting such an obscene litany. "Oh, fuck, shit cunt and piss!"

She heaved and groaned and pumped her ass up and down. Julia held on, one hand holding Jeanette's leg, the other hand holding the vibrator on Jeanette's twitching clit.

His fingers still inside her asshole, Harry pushed his thumb into her cunt-hole and began massaging the thin wall separating her cunt and ass. The new sensation carried her over the brink and she began

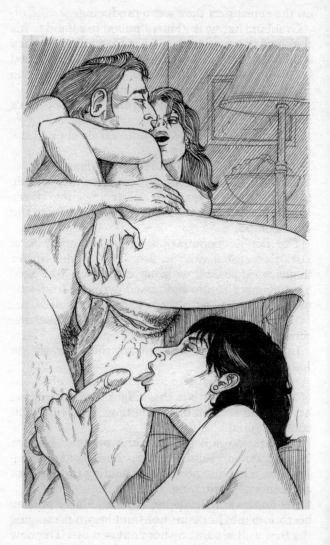

coming, her cunt convulsing and her legs shaking as the spasms hit her one after the other.

When it was finally over, she heard Julia say, "Let me watch you fuck her."

In a daze, she let them position her on her knees. Harry dropped his pants and moved in behind her. Julia remained beside her, playing with Jeanette's tits and ass, getting her ready for the fucking.

"She's lovely, Harry," Julia said. "I don't blame you at all."

Then Jeanette felt Harry's cock pushing into her cunt. Her cunt was still swollen and dripping, and his long thick cock eased into it. She groaned at the delicious sensation.

She felt Julia's hand playing in the spot where cock and cunt met. She could feel Julia's fingers squeezing her cunt lips, tightening them around Harry's cock-shaft.

Now Julia moved her hand to Jeanette's ass and put her fingers on Jeanette's asshole. Jeanette groaned as Julia tickled the tight hole. Harry continued pumping his cock in and out of her cunt, stroking her cunt-channel with his throbbing fuck-pole.

"Now give it to her in the ass!" Julia said, her voice low and urgent. "I want to see you buggering the horny bitch!"

Jeanette remained crouched over on the sofa on her knees, her head resting on her forearms, her ass raised up in the air as Julia greased up her asshole with cunt juice.

She was trembling uncontrollably now, her cunt going into endless spasms as she moved from one orgasm to the next. She was aware of Harry and Julia talking, but she couldn't make sense out of what they were saying and she didn't much care.

Then she felt Harry's fat cock-head pushing against her tight asshole. A moment later he drilled in, sinking his long thick cock deep into her rectum.

She was soon coming again, sobbing with pleasure at the way Julia pulled at her stiff nipples each time Harry thrust forward with his cock in her ass.

Then just as Harry started to tense and squirt a sperm enema up her backside, Julia shoved the vibrator inside Jeanette's cunt and she went wild. She cried out, she sobbed, and at the end she finally collapsed on the sofa in a trembling, twitching heap.

CHAPTER FIVE

At the very moment Jeanette's ass and cunt was receiving such superb attention from Harry and Julia, her husband was three hundred miles away getting turned on by a happy little blonde with big tits and a round ass. Her name was Dawn.

He had picked her up in a bar and now they were back in his hotel room and Warren Townsend had no doubt that he'd be able to fuck her without any trouble at all.

He liked these trips away from home. There were things he never felt comfortable doing with Jeanette that he always did with other women. Somehow he was inhibited with his wife. Maybe it was his religious upbringing. Fucking Jeanette was a duty. Fucking other women was a way to have a little fun.

Dawn seemed to be a girl who knew the score.

She looked about twenty, but he guessed she might be younger than that. He liked the way her firm tits were outlined against the tight sweater she was wearing.

She had stretched out on the bed, and now her legs were spread out at an angle. She sipped the Scotch out of her glass and smiled at him coquettishly.

"Cheers," Warren said, raising his glass to his lips.

Dawn giggled and showed him her pink tongue.

Sitting down on the bed, Warren put his hand on her knee and ran it up a few inches along the inside of her thigh.

"You've got a great body," he said.

She purred, "I've never had any complaints."

She spread her legs a bit more, and from where he was sitting Warren had a glimpse of blue panties and a few curls of blonde cunt hair.

She wiggled when his hand moved further up her thigh. He pushed her dress up until he could see her panties. His cock twitched as the intoxicating scent of hot pussy filled his nostrils.

He purred as he ran his fingertips over her crotch. Her pussy was damp to his touch. He could see the outline of her thick patch of cunt hair. She had a thick bush covering her clit mound. He'd never realized a blonde could be so hairy, and he was surprised. She's a hot cunted bitch, he thought.

Now she pushed her crotch forward, encouraging him to play with her cunt. He slipped a finger beneath the band of her panties and tickled her cunt bush. She trembled with pleasure at the first touch of his finger on her slit.

Squirming her ass on the bed, she told him in

a soft voice to take her pants off. "Do my pussy, lover," she whispered.

She watched him pull off her panties through narrowed eyes. He knew what she wanted.

Putting his hands on her thighs, he pushed them up and opened them to expose her crotch. He began kissing along the inside of her thighs, teasing her, enjoying the soft moans that escaped her lips. He gradually worked his face down to her crotch until he had his mouth hovering over her cunt. Blowing his hot breath on her meaty cunt-lips, he extended his tongue and began licking her.

She draped her legs over his shoulders and used her hands to pull his face into her cunt. His tongue probed through the forest of cunt hair to get at her cunt-lips. He teased her by staying away from her clit.

He lapped the meat of her pussy, burrowing between her thick cunt-lips, and then tickled the tip of his tongue over the sensitive skin between her cunt-hole and asshole.

"Oh, yeah, that's it!" she groaned.

A gasp came out of her throat when he finally closed hip lips over the bud of her swollen clit. He sucked hard on the quivering nub. Holding her ass-cheeks in his hands, he mashed his face into the wet meat of her pussy and massaged her clit with his nose and mouth and chin.

He liked a wet cunt. He could eat pussy all day. There were times when he wondered how Jeanette would react if he just pulled her pants down when he felt like it and simply started sucking her cunt. Dawn was obviously a girl who'd welcome that kind of attention any time she received it.

He stroked her asshole with his fingertip.

She squealed at the new sensation and pushed

her cunt more vigorously against his face.

"Suck me out!" she kissed. "Suck my pussy!"

He gobbled and slurped, scooping out her cunt juice with his tongue and swallowing it down. He swabbed the length of her cunt with his thick wet tongue. He chewed on her cunt-lips until they swelled up in his mouth.

"Oh, Jesus H. Christ!" she wailed. "You sure know how to give head!"

She gyrated her hips, humping her cunt up and down in a futile attempt to get more pressure on her clit.

"Oh, God, I can't take it any more!" she cried. "Fuck me! Let me have some cock!"

Warren pulled his face away from her dripping cunt, and chuckled. "Say that again," he smiled.

"I said *I want cock!*" she moaned.

He got up from the bed and teased her by undressing as slowly as possible. When he finally had his cock out, he fisted his cock-shaft and shook it at her.

"Is this what you want?"

"Oh, God, you're a bastard!" she giggled. "Fuck me before I scream!"

She reached out to grab him, but he backed away.

He looked down at her and grinned. Except for the fact that her dress was rolled up to her waist and her panties were off, she still had all her clothes on. Her wet cunt looked swollen and ready. When she saw the direction of his glance, she giggled again and opened her thighs even further.

"Come and get it!" she crooned. "Fuck that sweet prick into my box!"

He was turned on by the hot passion in her eyes.

He thought about Jeanette. Occasionally, he had seen that look in her eyes, but somehow it always embarrassed him.

In a way it was strange. He accepted, and was aroused by, the lust in the eyes of this girl, but not in the eyes of his wife.

"Oh, jeez, hurry!" Dawn groaned. "Your cock is dripping! I can see it. Get down here and fuck me!"

Pulling her legs up, she ran her hands down the insides of her thighs and framed her cunt with her fingers. Warren watched as she pulled her cunt-lips open and showed him the pink and red meat of her pussy.

"Bring it here, lover!" she purred.

When he deliberately hesitated, she leaned over to the edge of the bed and knelt in front of him. Her lips were just inches away from his cock-head. Her tongue slid out to swirl lightly over the head of his prick.

Closing his fist around his cock-shaft, he rubbed the knob of his cock against the side of her face. "Eat it!" he said. "Suck on it a little!"

She crooned with delight as she curled her fingers around his thick cock-shaft. When she attempted to pull his knob into her mouth, he laughed and stopped her by moving away.

"Take your clothes off," he said. "Strip everything off if you're going to suck me, I want you naked!"

She hurried to obey him. She quickly stripped all her clothes off and lay back on the bed. Her tits were fantastic. They were firm and full and her pink nipples were tight and hard with passion.

She was totally uninhibited. Moving one hand to her tits, she slipped the other hand between her thighs and began fingering her open gaping cunt.

"If you don't want to fuck me, I'll do it myself!" she teased.

He slowly pumped his cock as he watched her masturbate. She was a wild young thing. Someday she would settle down and get married. She would raise a house full of kids and get fat. Now she was horny and pretty, and the only thing she had on her mind was her craving for cock.

He grunted with approval as she pushed two fingers inside her cunt-hole and then pulled them out slick with her cunt juice. With a soft moan, she rubbed her cunt juice over her nipples and then returned her hand to her pussy.

"You're getting yourself all worked up," he teased. "I thought you wanted some cock!"

She moaned as she rapidly pumped her fingers in and out of her stretched cunt-hole.

"Oh, God, I'm so hot!" she cried.

He climbed onto the bed. Crouching over her, he straddled her chest and eased his weight down slowly so that his cock was nestled in the valley between her tits.

"I'm going to fuck your tits!" he said.

"Oh, yes, do it! Fuck them hard!"

He began gently however. He eased his cock-meat through the deep crease between her tits, feeling the soft flesh against his hairy balls. He pinched her nipples as he humped her tits, tugging and twirling the pink points until she moaned with pleasure.

Putting her hand on his ass, she pulled him into her, driving his cock harder between her tits. He held back. He wanted to tease her. He had an idea that teasing turned her on.

Her eyes were on the dripping red knob of his cock as it slipped in and out of the groove between her big firm melons.

"Oh, God, I like this," she groaned. "How does it feel?"

"It's almost as good as a cunt," he laughed. "You've got hot tits! Only a woman with hot tits can give a good tit fuck!"

"Don't come!" she wailed. "I want your cock in my cunt!"

He continued stroking his fuck-pole back and forth between the warm globes of her tits. He had never done anything like this to Jeanette. He had thought about it, but he couldn't imagine that Jeanette would ever go for it.

The cock juice dripping out of his piss-hole had now made the groove between Dawn's tits slippery. He squirmed his balls against her wet skin as he pumped his cock in and out of the velvety channel. It was good. A long time had passed since he'd fucked a pair of tits as pretty as these, and he had a yearning to drag it out as long as possible.

The yearning soon changed to a yearning to come. He knew she was hot to have his cock in her cunt, but he decided that what he really wanted was to shoot his load in her face. Fuck her! He thought. If she were afraid of getting a load of jism in her face, she would have stopped the tit fucking a long time ago.

He began speeding up his pumping, stroking his cock quickly in and out of the hot channel between her tits. She soon realized his intentions. Instead of pushing him away, she kept her eyes fixed on his sliding bloated cock-head and opened her mouth.

He looked down at her and shivered with lust. She had her mouth open as wide as possible and a look of hungry expectation on her face.

He soon felt the hot come begin to rise in his balls as they slapped down on her heaving tits. He groaned as he suddenly began spurting. The first gob of hot jism splashed on her forehead right above her eyes, and dripped down over her nose and cheeks.

The sight of his cream on her pretty face soon had him pumping in a frenzy to drain his balls. Each time he shot off, her tongue reached out to slurp up his thick come.

He sprayed her with his cock juice until his balls were drained. He watched her as she licked up the sticky juice with her pink tongue. The lovely sight kept his cock hard as a rock.

Easing his weight off her body, he ran his finger over her face and smeared his jism over her lips and mouth. She licked up his cream like a starved kitten.

She reached under him to fondle his balls and cock. She still wanted his cock, but he denied it to her.

"Give it to me!" she moaned. "Stick it into my cunt!"

He laughed, getting up on his knees and looking down at her. Crouching over her, he rubbed his cock over her face.

"Suck it a little to keep it hot!" he said.

"I want it in my pussy!" she pleaded.

"Suck it! Take it in your mouth!"

She finally opened her mouth and sucked in his throbbing cock-meat. She began tonguing his cock-head, sucking with a skill born of long practice.

He could feel another load of jism beginning to build inside his balls. As she sucked his cock, he moved his hand behind and found her hard little clit with his fingers. She moaned arid squirmed to encourage him.

"Just keep sucking!" he said.

He rocked his hips gently back and forth in rhythm with her eager sucking. His cock made a slurping sound as it thrust in and out of her wet mouth. Her lips were still slippery with his jism. Her hand tickled his hairy balls, urging him forward.

She was an expert at giving head. She kept her lips curled over her teeth to keep from nicking the sensitive skin of his cock. She was able to take his big cock all the way down into her throat without gagging. She obviously was an experienced cocksucker.

"Keep at it!" he said. "You're doing fine!" He was pumping now, fucking her face with a steady rhythm, shoving his cock furiously in and out of the wet ring of her lips and gazing down at the junction of mouth and cock.

"Suck it, baby! Suck it all out!"

She was aware now that he was going to shoot his load into her mouth. She obviously wanted it. She nodded her head wildly up and down, urging him on.

"You like the taste of hot come, don't you?" he said, his voice condescending.

She resisted the temptation of biting down and simply answered by pressing her lips more tightly around his cock. Her hand slid up from his balls and stroked his wet cock-shaft each time it came out of her clinging mouth. There was anticipation in her eyes. She was waiting for the fresh load of cock juice that he would send pouring down her throat.

"Soon!" he groaned. •

He grabbed a handful of her hair and pulled her head back and forth to make her speed up the rhythm of her sucking. She loved it! As her eyes clouded with a mixture of pain and pleasure, he pumped his bursting cock deep into her throat and started coming.

Spurt after spurt of cock juice jetted into her eager mouth. He kept his cock moving until he had drained his balls. She panted, gasping for breath, and when it seemed as though she might choke on his jism, he pulled his wet prick out of her dripping mouth and rolled over on the bed.

"You're a hot-cunted bitch!" he groaned. "Suck it hard again and I'll fuck your pussy!"

It didn't take long. She sucked his cock with her ass sticking in his face, and the sight of her lovely white ass-cheeks soon had his prick stiff again.

He made her kneel on the edge of the bed with her ass in the air. Standing behind her, he rammed his cock into her drenched cunt without any delay. She needed no further priming. Her pussy was aching for his cock.

Holding her ass-cheeks in his hands, he pushed his cock in all the way to the hilt with one thrust. She groaned with pleasure. A guttural wail came out of her throat.

"Fuck me! Give it to me hard!"

"Say pretty please!"

"Pretty please!"

"Okay," he chuckled.

He began ramming his cock in and out of her frothing cunt. She was soon grunting, making the same guttural sounds she'd made before, her nails clawing the sheet. He pumped her with smooth hard strokes until she began coming.

He could feel the tickly sensations in his balls that heralded an imminent ejaculation. When he felt the spasms in her pussy, he let go and gave her his last load. He shuddered as he spurted into her cunt. With a loud grunt, he rammed his cock into her pussy one last time and then slumped onto the bed and closed his eyes.

CHAPTER SIX

"Come one inside the office," the man said. His name was Phil Avramidis. To his peers he was simply known as 'Phil the Greek'. He was a big man with jet black, slicked back hair, big hands and a big cigar in his mouth. He wore a tailored black suit and an immaculately ironed white shirt open to reveal a broad, hairy chest and two or three thick gold chains. He owned a place called the White Tower Club. Jeanette had seen the ad in the paper for a cashier, and she was anxious to get the job. She was fed up with Harry and Julia Baker. It was too dangerous playing games like that with people who knew Warren. What she needed was a way to have some fun on her own. Warren said he wouldn't mind her working at night as long as it wasn't on weekends.

"You're too pretty to be a cashier," Avramidis said. He had a deep, gravely voice that seemed to rumble from somewhere in the depths of his chest.

Jeanette blushed. "Thank you."

"I've got a better-paying job for you, if you want it."

"Oh?"

"I run a private little poker game on Monday

and Thursday nights. I need a girl to take care of the booze and order sandwiches. I'll pay you a hundred bucks a night."

"Oh, wow!"

He laughed at the look of astonishment on her face. "There's a catch," he said. "You go topless."

Jeanette shook her head vehemently. "No. I can't do that."

"Why not?"

"I have a husband."

"So what? The game is very private. These guys are big shots. Your husband doesn't have to know a thing. You'll make good money and the work is easy. There's no rough stuff. Nobody lays a hand on you. The last girl who had the job had a husband and two kids. I was damn sorry to lose her, but her husband got transferred. I don't like young kids in that job. There's too much going on. I need someone who knows the score."

He chewed on his big cigar and raked his eyes over her tits and legs.

She was tempted. For some inexplicable reason, her pussy started to get very wet at the idea of exhibiting herself like that to strangers. She'd wanted a job to have some fun, but this sounded like too much fun, somehow. At least fun that was too dangerous.

Avramidis saw her hesitation and smiled. "You don't have to fuck anyone – not unless you want to."

"All right," she said with a brave smile, "I'll try it."

"Good!" he smiled. "Why don't you take your clothes off and let me have a look at that you've got."

She froze. Then she realized it made sense. He intended to pay her a hundred dollars a night to show her body, and he had a right to see what she looked like. It was business. It was no different than being a model.

She stripped off her clothes without any attempt to tease him, but by the time she finished undressing down to her panties, her pussy was wet and she was turned on by the lust in his eyes as he looked her over. She wondered if he could see the darker patch of fabric where her juices had seeped.

"Nice tits!" he said.

The young housewife trembled when he put his hands on her shoulders. She knew she ought to protest, but she remained motionless while he ran his fingers over her ass and hips and finally closed his big beefy hands over the melons of her tits.

He chuckled when she moaned. "You like to fuck, don't you?"

Jeanette remained silent. He asked her again.

"Yes," she whispered. It was an admission she found humiliating.

"That's nothing to be ashamed of. I like to fuck too, so how about that?"

Moving away from her, he quickly stripped his clothes off. He opened the convertible sofa to reveal a bed. His big red cock throbbed. He pulled her down onto the bed and went to work on her.

He leaned over her and began licking her swollen tits. He sucked and chewed on her hard nipples until they glistened with his saliva. Moving his head down over her belly, he nuzzled his face into her cunt-hair. She writhed at the sensations made by his mouth and nose in her crotch.

"Oh, yes!" she groaned. "I love to have my

pussy licked! Eat me!"

She moved her legs apart. He slipped his head between her thighs, snorting and sniffing the aroma of her cunt, his tongue fluttering over her thick wet cunt-lips.

He probed the hot rim of her cunt-mouth. He licked around the opening and then pushed his tongue inside. She quivered as he briefly tongue-fucked her cunt-hole.

Then he pulled his tongue out and moved it up to her turgid clit. He massaged the swollen little button until cunt juice gushed out of her cunt-hole in a small flood.

Her legs pulled back, her thighs opened, she marvelled at the strangeness of it all. Just a short time ago she hadn't even known this man. Now his face was between her legs and he was sucking voraciously at her pussy!

He sucked like an expert. He knew how to use all of his face to massage the steaming hot swamp of her cunt. His nose vibrated against her clit while his thick tongue pistonned in and out of her cunt-hole.

Phil draped her legs over his shoulders and held her thighs in his big hands. Occasionally she craned her neck to look down at his head. She loved the feel of a man's head between her thighs. She loved the feel of a man's mouth sucking her oozing pussy. The feel of his tongue pumping in and out of her dripping cunt-hole was exquisite.

She squirmed her ass, bucking her hips, grinding her cunt in his face. They soon found a common rhythm. He sucked and rubbed and chewed to the same tempo as the movement of her thrusting hips.

"Roll over!" he grunted.

He made Jeanette kneel on the bed with her head down and her ass up in the air. She wiggled her hips. She thought he was going to fuck her, but he had something else in mind.

Crouching behind her, he began running his tongue over the smooth skin of her ass-cheeks. She groaned when she felt his wet tongue running into the crack of her ass.

His tongue fluttered over the sensitive stretch of skin between her asshole and pussy hole. The sensation was incredible. The crack of her ass was soon soaked with his saliva.

His tongue gradually neared the tight puckered ring of her asshole, and soon he zeroed in on it. He licked around the rim. He massaged the muscle. Then he stiffened his tongue and pushed it forward until it slithered inside her clenched shit-hole.

A wail came out of her throat as he began pistonning his tongue in and out of her quivering bunghole.

"Oh, God!" she moaned.

He gave a throaty chuckle.

"Not quite. But they say I'm not bad..."

Her hips gyrated and deep groans came out of her throat. He continued pumping his tongue in and out of her asshole, and then he suddenly pulled it out and rammed his finger into the hot grip of her shit-tube.

"Sweet little ass!" was all he could say, over and over again, as if he couldn't quite believe what he was seeing.

She thought he was about to fuck her in the ass, but instead he pushed her over on her back again and straddled her chest. The swollen head of his cock dangled directly over her face.

He grinned down at her. "Open up honey!"

She gobbled up as much of his cock as she could into her mouth. She swirled her tongue over his bloated cock-head. She tickled his piss-hole with the tip of her tongue, licking up the cock juice oozing out.

The swarthy nightclub owner began rocking back and forth, slowly pumping his cock in and out of her mouth as she continued sucking and slurping on his turgid fuck-meat.

"You're a juicy fuck!" he grunted. "I could tell the minute I laid eyes on you!"

She moaned in response. Shifting forward, he began driving his cock more deeply into her throat. She could feel the swelling and throbbing of his cock-shaft. She could feel the pulsating in his cock-head. Waves of lust rolled over her body as she sucked on his swollen prick. She tried not to gag as his cock went deeper than she'd ever taken one before. She concentrated on relaxing her throat and her breathing.

He tangled his fingers in her hair. Reaching behind him, he squeezed and pulled at Jeanette's jiggling tits. A wheeze came out of his throat as he looked down at her sucking lips.

"You're good!" he said. "You're very good!"

His cock plunged in and out of her face relentlessly. She wanted him to pump a load of jism down her throat, but she also wanted to be fucked. The ramming of his cock in and out of her mouth made her tremble with lust. Her clit demanded attention.

She clutched the meat of her pussy with her hand, probing her yawning cunt-hole with her fingers and strumming her stiff clit with her thumb. A flood of cunt juice oozed out of her pussy as his cock pounded in and out of her sucking lips.

Her crotch was soaked. She had juice covering her cunt and leaking down to the crack of her ass. There was a puddle of it on the sheet under her body. God, how I love this, she thought. She was getting as much out of it as he was.

Her heavy tits bounced like ripe grapefruit as he shot his fuck-pole in and out of her throat. She could feel herself moving closer and closer to the brink of an orgasm. She could feel the rippling of her cunt-walls. She mewled with delight when she felt the cock-head in her mouth swell.

The big Greek rammed harder and then suddenly his cock exploded. His jism blasted out in thick jets. She had no choice but to swallow it. Again and again she swallowed in order to avoid choking. A river of jism washed over her teeth and tongue and flowed down her throat. She drank him down in great gulps.

"Drink it! Drink it down, baby!" he said. "Drink it all!"

She sucked and swallowed and slurped, draining his balls, milking his fat cock-head until there was nothing left. When he finally pulled his cock out of her mouth, she was astonished to see that his cock was still pretty hard.

"You want some fucking?"

"Oh, God, yes!" she groaned.

Phil crawled between her open thighs. She closed her hand around the thick shaft of his cock and positioned his cock-head at the mouth of her brimming cunt-hole. She rubbed his knob against the juicy hot meat of her cunt-lips.

With a lurch forward he drove his throbbing cock into her juice-drenched fuck-channel. A moan of pleasure came out of her throat. She bucked her ass up as he slid further into her cunt-hole.

She let out a squeal of pleasure as her cunt-lips closed tightly around the hard thick shaft of his cock. His cock was big and thick and it felt marvellous. Her hands clutched at his ass as his fat cock-head reamed into her cunt-channel. Her pussy felt deliciously stretched.

She could feel his jism-bloated balls tickling her ass. In a moment she was completely penetrated by his long, thick fuck-pole. She loved the feeling of being impaled by a big thick slab of cock-meat, loved the feeling of her vagina stretched around his meaty cock-shaft. She felt deliciously stuffed.

He had worked her up to a fever pitch, and now she was ready for the hard fucking she knew he could give her.

With a grunt, Avramidis began screwing his big cock around and around. Jeanette squirmed from side to side, grinding her pussy against his cock-meat. She could hear the squishing of her cunt juice as he moved his prick in and out of her wet hole.

He fucked her with a steady rhythm, his muscular ass pumping up and down as he thrust his cock back and forth in her hot dripping cunt. He ploughed her tight, clasping pussy. The delicious feeling of it drove her wild. She trembled and quaked with the force of each thrust. His hot cock-flesh rubbed against her tingling cunt-flesh. The slurping sound of cock sliding in and out of cunt filled the air.

His balls smacked lustily against her ass. Cunt juice gushed out of her to smear the cheeks of her ass and soak the sheet.

"Oh, fuck me silly!" she groaned. "Oh, how lovely..."

She screwed her juice-filled cunt up and down

on his cock. "Fuck me hard!" she groaned. "Give it to me!"

He screwed her with long hard strokes. The bed creaking, her body shaking, she pumped her ass furiously to fuck back at his plunging cock. Her long stiff nipples rubbed against his chest. Her ripe heavy tits jiggled. Their wet bellies slapped noisily together.

The wild tempo of their fucking soon brought her to the brink. She tossed her head wildly from side to side, urging him on.

"Fuck my cunt!" she begged. "Ram it in!" Her legs waved crazily in the air as he continued pounding his cock with piston-like thrusts in and out of her juice-filled hole. Each savage thrust made her body quake. She wailed and groaned as his cock and balls pounded her crotch.

Now she could feel her climax approaching. She drew her knees back. She pulled her legs up and draped them over his shoulders.

"Fuck me harder!" she screamed.

Her thighs slid down and she pounded her heels into the crack of his ass, beating his ass with her feet. She was like a wild animal in heat. He battered her cunt without mercy and still she wanted more.

Her legs were up high. Her knees were now pulled back against her shoulders. The saddle of her crotch was open to him. She offered him the full length of her hairy juice-drenched cunt.

Again and again, he lurched forward to bury his cock in her hairy slippery hole. The pounding thrusts made her body shudder. Her grasping sucking cunt fucked up and down over the thick length of his hard cock-shaft.

"Oh, God, I'm coming!" she wailed.

Her lips pulled back in a grimace of lust as her face contorted with pleasure. The orgasm was overwhelming. Her cunt exploded. Her hips grated as she ground her pussy up and down on his pile-driving cock.

A moment later he grunted as his thick hot jism began gushing into her spasming fuck hole. They clung frantically to each other until they were drained. When Avramidis finally rolled off her, he tickled her lightly and chuckled.

"I just knew you were a juicy little nympho!" he said with a grin.

You're right, thought Jeanette ruefully.

CHAPTER SEVEN

Jeanette's first night as a hostess at Phil Avramidis's private poker game occurred a week later.

She trembled with apprehension when the day arrived. She had stage fright. She wondered how she'd ever have the nerve to go topless in front of strangers. It was crazy. She was certain that after five minutes of it she would lose her cool and have to quit the job.

But it turned out to be easier than she expected.

Phil Avramidis was there, and that reassured her. At least with Phil there the men would keep their hands away from her tits.

The fact was that the first time she came out with her bare tits jigging, they hardly looked at her. They were there to play poker. They were used to having bare-titted girls in the room, and she quickly learned that they considered her tits less interesting than a good poker hand.

She was relieved, but deep down she was a little peeved. She had expected more attention.

Phil had made her wear a mini-skirt with a garter-belt and black stockings, and he told her she looked sexy as hell. She felt that way. The crotch of her black lace panties was soaked five minutes after she put them on.

It made no difference. At the end of the first hour of the poker game, she had resigned herself to being nothing more than a pair of hands bringing booze and food to the table. Even Phil ignored her. He was too busy playing the game.

At the end of the second hour, Phil left the game and came into the kitchen to find out how she was doing.

He cupped her naked tits in his hands and told her the men thought she was a real looker. She was pleased. At least they'd noticed!

She thought Phil would fuck her right there in the kitchen, but he did no more than stick his finger in her pussy. When she asked for more, he chuckled and told her that two of the men wanted to see her after the game broke up at midnight.

"I couldn't do that," she said.

"Why not?" he insisted. "Think it over."

She thought it over. She knew the men wanted to fuck her. Their names were Berlotti and Herzog. They were local politicians. They were men used to getting what they wanted and she shivered at the idea of getting fucked by two of them. Maybe they would fuck her at the same time. Imagining that brought a gush of hot cunt juice out of her pussy.

At the end of the third hour she whispered to

Phil that she'd be willing to go with the two men when the poker game ended.

"Good little girl!" Phil laughed. He patted her ass and playfully pinched her nipples.

Berlotti was a tall thin man with rimless eyeglasses. Dark-haired and sallow-skinned. Herzog had a pink complexion and a stocky body. They smiled when Jeanette told them she had to be home by two in the morning. Her husband would fume if she got home later than that.

"Don't worry your pretty little head," Berlotti said.

The way his hands fondled her ass, she was sure he had no interest in her head at all.

They took her to a motel. By the time they were inside the room, she was trembling with eagerness.

When Herzog went out to get a bottle of bourbon and ice, she moved into Berlotti's arms. His hands fondling her ass-cheeks, Berlotti grinned.

"You're a hot little piece!"

She could feel his cock growing stiff. She rubbed her tits back and forth across his chest. Her nipples were long and hard, and now they tingled from the friction. She pressed her belly against his hard-on and wondered briefly if he was married.

"I had my eye on you all night," he breathed, his fingers clutching the cheeks of her ass.

"I was sure you didn't really take any notice of me," Jeanette said, attempting to answer in kind. She began unbuttoning his shirt.

"You first," he laughed. "Let me have a look at those tits again!"

When she peeled off her blouse, he smiled at the way her dark nipples showed through the transparent material of her bra. This time there was no poker game. She had all his attention and, to her surprise, she was loving it!

Teasing him, she unhooked her bra slowly and let it fall away to expose her heaving boobs. He put his hands under her tits, hefting their weight and lifting them up.

Lowering his head, he took a hard nipple between his lips. He sucked her tit like a starving glutton. She moaned as his teeth scraped over the nipple. He held the globe of tit-flesh with both hands and stuffed it into his mouth.

He swabbed his tongue back and forth, exciting the turgid knob even further. Then he moved from one tit to the other and continued sucking until both nipples were red and swollen.

Herzog entered the room with a bottle of bourbon in his hands and his eyes wide at the sight of Berlotti working over Jeanette's tits.

"I've got two!" she said playfully, "so why don't you come over and help?"

How lewd she was! She knew she was acting crazy, but the idea that she would soon be fucking both of them drove her wild.

A big grin on his face, Herzog locked the door. When he turned around again, their eyes met. She licked her lips suggestively. He leered and began loosening his belt.

A moment later his pants dropped down around his ankles and she could see the bulge of his cock in his jockey shorts. She licked her lips again, her fingers running through Berlotti's hair as he continued sucking on her tit.

Herzog peeled his shorts down and exposed a thick dripping cock.

"Oh, I like that!" she said, speaking low, surprised

by the intensity of her own voice.

Berlotti's greedy sucking was making her pussy quiver. He had one of his hands under her skirt and his fingers were climbing between her thighs to her crotch. Her legs trembled what his fingertips began stroking her wet pussy.

Now he peeled her panties dawn and she stepped out of them. She could feel the heat in her cunt. It felt almost as though steam were escaping from her cunt when she opened her legs!

Herzog was holding his thick tan cock-shaft in his hand and slowly jerking it up and down. She watched him with fascinated eyes. He stroked his cock with a slow deliberate motion, his eyes fixed on her stiff-nippled, swaying tits.

"You want to suck my cock?" Herzog asked.

"Yes!" she gasped.

Berlotti rose up and the two men finished stripping off their clothes. Then Berlotti came to stand behind her. He reached around and held her tits in his hands. He pressed his hard cock against the checks of her ass. Then he worked at the zipper of her skirt and let it drop down so that she could step out of it.

The three of them were naked now. "Come on, baby!" Herzog said, waving his cock at her. "It's waiting for you! My prick wants to fill that pretty little mouth of yours! Come and get it!"

He stood where he was, taunting her to come after his cock. She gazed with lust at his muscular body and his thick throbbing prick.

Her tits heaving, she moved to him and leaned down, bending at the waist, bringing her lips to the head of his bloated cock.

She teased him by blowing her hot breath over his spongy cock-head. She could see a clear drop of cock-juice brimming in the slit of his piss-hole. Extending her tongue, she touched her tongue-tip to the drop of juice and slurped it up into her mouth.

Then she smacked her lips, opened them again, and took all of his swollen cock-head into her mouth. At first she just held his cock there, not moving her lips or her tongue. Then she began swabbing her tongue over the tight skin of his cock-head. She revelled in the slightly salty taste of his cock-meat. Thick juice oozed out of her cunt as she sucked on his prick.

Berlotti was standing behind her naked, bent-over body. He crouched down on his knees and began kissing the checks of her ass. She squirmed with pleasure, wriggling her soft, womanly asscheeks against his face. She loved the feel of his rough beard against her tender skin.

She knew that bending forward as she was, her cunt and ass were completely exposed to him. She could feel him sniffing at her. The lewdness of it made her tremble. The tremble became a shudder when she felt his wet tongue spearing her tight asshole.

Herzog's cock muffled the mewling sound that came out of her throat. Berlotti's tongue was driving her crazy! She quickly reached back to pull open her buttocks and give him better access to her asshole, and a moment later his tongue slithered inside like a hot eel. She moaned at the way it wriggled inside her shit hole.

She had her asshole filled with a tongue and her mouth filled with a cock. The pleasure of it was exquisite. She continued sucking Herzog's cock as Berlotti's tongue explored her ass. He soon had his tongue pumping in and out of her shit-hole, reaming out the raised ring.

She threw her ass back at his face to encourage him. She rocked back and forth, forcing his tongue to move in and out of her asshole like a pile-driving cock.

At the same time she bobbed her mouth up and down on Herzog's hard prick.

Reaching out now for Herzog's balls, she rolled his nuts around in her hand and then snaked a finger behind his ball-bag to his asshole. He grunted as she tickled the rim of his brownie.

Berlotti continued lapping eagerly at her bung. Then he nuzzled her wet asshole with his nose and lowered his head to get his tongue inside her pussy.

She mewled and quivered as he began driving his tongue in and out of her cunt. It wasn't long before she shuddered and came.

"Oooohhh, yeah!" she wailed.

Wave after wave of spasms shot through her. She quivered and trembled, pumping her ass back at Berlotti's face. Her legs felt as if they were made of rubber and would give way at the least provocation.

He continued licking the outside of her cunt, slurping up her cunt juice, until she started coming again.

"Uunnngghhh! Oh, God!" she wailed. "Sweet Mother of God!"

Herzog's cock dropped out of her mouth. She straightened up. "My back hurts," she groaned.

She lay down on the bed with her legs spread. Herzog crouched at the lower end of her body and gazed appreciatively at her wide-open gaping cunt, hair matted with cunt juice.

Berlotti climbed onto the bed behind her with

his crotch hanging over her face. She opened her mouth, inviting his cock. He dropped his hips and a moment later she had his fat cock-head inside her pulsating lips.

As she sucked on his bloated prick, she felt Herzog pulling her cunt-lips completely open. She drew up her knees to expose her crotch to him better. He moved in between her thighs, and a moment later she felt his thick cock push forward into the narrow, tight channel of her vagina.

Now she had two cocks inside her. Herzog buried his cock to the hilt in her cunt, and Berlotti buried his cock to the hilt in her mouth.

She had Berlotti's balls resting on her nose and Herzog's balls resting on her ass.

Her clit quivered and throbbed as Herzog's thick cock-shaft scraped against it. She arched her back, asking for more.

Berlotti pumped his hips, fucking her mouth with his cock as though her mouth were a cunt. Both men played with her tits.

She thrashed around hungrily. The feeling of being stuffed with cock fore and aft was incredible. She writhed and squirmed on the bed. How lovely it was to have her cunt filled at the same time as her mouth was filled with lovely male meat!

She knew the friction of Herzog's cock against her clit would soon bring her off. They were moving to the same rhythm now, pumping her cunt and mouth in unison.

"Christ what a slut!" Herzog said, his voice somewhere between a wheeze and a gasp.

His words thrilled her. Yes, she was a slut! Damn her husband! She had two cocks in her now, and she loved them both!

Berlotti's fat cock-head rammed mercilessly

into her throat each time he lurched forward. She rolled her hips to get more of Herzog's prick in her cunt.

Slurping noises came out of her cunt and mouth as she sucked hungrily at the two cocks at the two ends of her body.

"Oh, Jesus!" Herzog grunted. "Baby, here comes a hot load for you! Oh, fuck!"

Jeanette felt spurt after spurt of Herzog's thick jism shooting into her cunt. She loved the slippery feel of it. Her pussy flooded with his white cream and the excess dripped out, soaking the puckered rim of her asshole.

She trembled as she started coming again. Her tits heaved. She clamped her mouth down on Berlotti's cock as her body convulsed, and then he started coming. The first blast of his jism shot directly down her throat. She caught the second on the side of her face.

He quickly aimed at her mouth and soon filled it with his thick hot cream. She swallowed and licked and swallowed again.

The two cocks finally slipped out of her body. Her cunt and mouth were slippery with cunt-juice and jism. Licking her lips, she rolled over and closed her eyes. Berlottie slumped back onto the bed. But Herzog wanted more. He was slightly drunk and wanted to prove to this pretty young housewife what a stud he was. He dragged her to the bathroom and asked her to suck him. When this failed to produce an erection for him, he said, "Let's do something else. Ever tried golden showers?"

Jeanette had no idea what he meant, but not wanting to appear an ingénue, she nodded vaguely. To her surprise, Herzog lay down in the empty tub.

"Now squat on top of me and let it all go," he said, chuckling. Slightly uncertain of what she was meant to be doing, Jeanette got into position and looked down at the corpulent politician.

"You mean…"

"Yes, honey, I want you to piss all over me. C'mon… get those waterworks going!"

Hiding her distaste for such a puerile game, Jeanette tried to pee, but even though she had a full bladder, she was unable to give Herzog anything other than the sperm he had so recently deposited inside her, which splattered over the fat man's lower stomach at the same time as her pussy released some trapped air with a little farting sound. Jeanette reddened with embarrassment. Herzog chuckled and turned on one of the faucets with his toes. The sound of water had the desired effect and suddenly Jeanette was pissing, gushing uncontrollably all over his plump form.

"That's the ticket… good girl…" he gasped ecstatically as she obliged him in his perverted pleasures and the golden shower rained down on him. By now he was hard enough for her to sit down on him, impaling herself on his cock. As she rose and fell, she could smell the faint ammoniacal odour that her urine gave off. It seemed Herzog only wanted to receive, not to give in this curious exchange of bodily fluids. She was relieved, but a more prurient part of her mind wondered what it would be like to be pissed on. After she was done they showered together and she soaped his stiff cock until it spat out a few weak jets of cum. They dried off and joined

Berlotti on the bed, utterly exhausted.

When she opened her eyes again, Berlotti and Herzog had gone. She groaned. She wondered what time it was, and then decided she didn't care. It would do Warren a power of good to worry about her.

She'd spent the evening fucking and sucking two strange men as a result of his neglect. One of them asked me to urinate on him and she had. She had found two fifty-dollar bills on the bedside table, the implication of which had doubled her resolve to quit this her association with the White Tower Club. No, I can't go on like this, she thought.

She knew that if she continued working for Phil Avramidis, she would soon be fucking every man in the poker game and only God knew what other perverts. And she might become too used to receiving those 'tips'.

She had to stop it. As much as she wanted the sex, this quasi-prostitution was no way to get it. She was destroying herself. There had to be another way. And she was determined to find it.

CHAPTER EIGHT

Jeanette withdrew from the world. She wanted nothing more to do with either Harry Baker or Phil Avramidis. She stayed in the house as much as possible. She read or watched television day and night.

Warren realized there was something wrong, but when he asked her about it she told her she was just down in the dumps and that it would pass.

What she really needed was a chance to talk to someone. Her next-door neighbour was a woman named Kate Dunmore. Kate was about ten years older than Jeanette. Kate was mild-mannered and kind. She wore her lovely reddish-blonde hair short and round, gold-rimmed spectacles, which gave her a slightly schoolmarmish appearance. She was active in one of the local church groups. Jeanette had always thought Kate was a sympathetic soul. She decided that if she had to talk to someone, she would talk to Kate. Kate would understand.

And so one day Jeanette got up in the morning resolved that this would be the day she would pour her heart out to Kate Dunmore.

She put it off as long as possible. She powdered and primped and waited an hour trying to decide what to wear. She finally realized she was just delaying things, and she threw on a pair of slacks and a jersey top and crossed the yard to the back door of Kate's house.

There was a milk truck parked in the Dunmore driveway. Jeanette knew that Kate's husband was out of town at some religious convention. She tried to remember if anyone in Kate's family was a milkman. It couldn't be! Jeanette thought. Surely nothing that corny...

Then she heard a moan coming from one of the back windows, and her heart pounded with excitement as she realized what was going on.

She hesitated, torn between the urge to see and the knowledge that it would be wrong. The urge won out.

She moved as quietly as possible to the kitchen window. There was enough space between the curtains so that she was able to peer into the room.

Kate was on her back on the kitchen table, her

golden hair spread out around her head like a halo. A man was facing her, holding her legs in his arms, and slowly but thoroughly fucking her.

Jeanette restrained a gasp. She had never imagined Kate capable of anything like this. The man certainly wasn't Kate's husband. Even if he were, Kate just wasn't the sort of woman that anyone would expect to find fucking the milkman on a kitchen table!

Mesmerized, Jeanette stared at the milkman's pumping ass. How thrilling it was to watch them! Jeanette's legs trembled as she realized how turned on she was. The heady excitement of watching people fuck drove her wild.

The couple in the kitchen shifted their positions a bit, and now for the first time Jeanette was able to get a good look at the junction of cock and cunt.

She held back a giggle when she saw that Kate's pussy was shaved. Kate was certainly full of surprises! It was difficult to believe that the moaning squirming woman being fucked on the kitchen table was actually Kate Dunmore.

Jeanette mused over how difficult it was to know what people were really like. She had always thought Kate was a prude. She'd never once heard Kate mention anything about sex. Now here was Kate having her bald little pussy worked over by the milkman!

Jeanette could see the milkman's swinging balls slapping against Kate's ass.

"Oh, Jesus, give it to me!" Kate groaned. The milkman began pumping more vigorously, pumping his cock in and out of Kate's hairless cunt.

Jeanette remained transfixed, her eyes wide, her

heart pounding with excitement. The milkman ran one hand over Kate's belly, fingering her tits and then her ass.

When his fingers moved underneath into the crack of Kate's ass, Kate moaned. The moan turned into a grunt when he suddenly drilled a finger into her tight asshole.

"Oh, yes!" Kate groaned. "Diddle my ass!"

"You like that, huh?" the milkman rasped.

"I love it!"

He finger-fucked her ass to the same tempo as the pounding of his cock in her pussy. Kate's ass-cheeks glistened with her cunt juice.

Holding her breath, Jeanette watched the pumping of the milkman's cock in and out of Kate's juice-drenched pussy.

"Coming soon?" he grunted.

"Yes!" Kate wailed. "Shoot it into me! Give it to me! Fuck me hard!"

Holding her legs in his arms, he began ramming his prick in and out of her cunt-channel in frenzy. The table shook under his thrusting.

Kate's big breasts vibrated like jelly. She wailed and moaned and quaked at the jackhammer thrusts of his fuck-pole.

"Oh, shit!" he cried out. "Uunnnggghhh!"

Her pussy quivering, Jeanette imagined the spurts of his come jetting into Kate's hot pussy. She watched the flexing of his ass cheeks as he drained his balls, tight in their scrotum.

Kate groaned and heaved up her body as she received his hot load. When he finally pulled out, Jeanette was shocked to see him suddenly crouch down and plaster his mouth against Kate's jism-filled cunt.

"Oh, God, yes!" Kate groaned. "Suck me out!

Eat me!"

With a grunt, the milkman began slurping up the cream he had so recently deposited in Kate's feverish cunt. He slurped and sucked until Kate tensed rigid and shook with another intense come.

Resting on her elbows, her neck craned up so that she could look down at him, Kate began pumping her crotch at the milkman's face as he continued sucking their combined juices as they oozed out of her cunt-hole.

When it was finally over, Jeanette was breathless. She leaned against the house a moment to recover her senses. Then she carefully stole away.

By the time she entered her own house, she was trembling with excitement and need. Her cunt was on fire.

She went directly to the bedroom and stripped off her clothes. Stretching out on the bed, she pushed three fingers inside her cunt hole and began a furious masturbation.

Her knees pulled back, her teeth clenched, she finger-fucked her pussy with a rapid rhythm. It was no good. She had a small orgasm, but it wasn't enough. She needed more. She needed a cock.

With a frustrated shudder, she pulled her hand out of her cunt and left the bed.

She decided to dress and go out. Somewhere in town there must be a place where she could pick up a man who would fuck her with no questions asked. She needed fucking so bad she would die if she didn't have it soon!

"My name's Merret," he said.

She found him in a hotel bar. He was young, maybe twenty-two or twenty-three. He had a deep tan, muscular arms, and a lazy knowing look. He told her she could rent him out for fifty bucks.

"You're kidding!" she said.

He shook his head and smiled. "No, I'm not."

"You mean you want me to pay you to go to bed with me?"

The more she thought about it, the more she liked the idea. This was certainly one way to have a man without any strings attached.

She had the money in her purse. She was tempted. "Are you any good?" she asked.

"I've never had any complaints!" he said. She lacked the nerve to take him home. Instead, she drove him to a motel. Halfway there, she reached over and put a hand on his cock. She squeezed and probed the bulge of his crotch. I'm paying for it, she thought. "I can't believe I'm really doing this!" she said.

He laughed, "You want my cock out?"

"Oh, Jesus!" she breathed.

Her eyes shifted back and forth between the road and his crotch. He soon had his cock out. His fuck-pole swayed with the movements of the car.

He spread his fly open so that she could see his balls. His ball-bag was a dark tan colour and hairy. The skin of his sac was wrinkled and ridged. His balls looked rock-hard.

She gaped at his cock. His cock-head looked as smooth as velvet, the skin tight and glistening. The knob was bloated. A bead of clear fluid brimmed in his piss-hole.

"Oh, God, put it away before someone sees us!" she said in an urgent whisper.

He chuckled. He seemed totally unconcerned about the passing cars. She wondered if anyone could see anything.

She gasped when he put his hand on her thigh and then moved his fingers up to press the bulge of her cunt.

"Stop it, please!" she moaned. "I can't drive like this!"

With a deep laugh he removed his hand from her crotch and stuffed his cock back into his pants.

"You're right," he said. "It's better to wait. I just wanted to give you a preview."

She could feel the wetness on the insides of her thighs as they drove up to the motel.

After registering, at the desk, she hurriedly drove the car around to the room.

Once inside, she locked the door and faced him. He grinned at her. He moved forward, closing his arms around her, pulling her against him.

Merret's mouth came down on hers and his tongue probed between her lips. She accepted the kiss. His hands moved over her back, kneading her flesh. Then one hand came, around to her tit and cupped it gently, squeezing it.

She groaned, and arched her body forward, pressing her belly against his hard cock. She could feel the bulge of his cock through the material of his pants.

They wriggled against each other, the outline of his prick sliding back and forth across her belly.

Fondling her clit with one hand, he moved the other hand down to her ass. His fingers gathered up her skirt, bunching it until her ass was exposed.

Slipping her panties down, he grabbed a full ass-cheek in his hand and squeezed it. "What would you like?"

She looked at him and quivered. "Suck my pussy!" she said, her eyes narrowing in raw lust.

He smiled. He began to undress her slowly.

He stripped her clothes off piece by piece, and each time a new part of her body was exposed he covered it with wet kisses.

Then he made her stretch out on the bed on her back with her legs pulled up. Kneeling down, he began kissing the insides of her thighs, gradually working his way towards her steaming crotch.

She groaned and trembled as his mouth approached her cunt. Her hot pussy had turned into a swamp of cunt juice.

"Suck it!" she crooned. "Lick my pussy!"

He nuzzled in. He swabbed the flat of his tongue up and down, pushing open her thick cunt-lips, tickling the rim of her cunt-hole, and fluttering over her stiff little clit.

She spread her legs as wide as possible, shivering with delight. Whimpering sobs of pleasure came out of her throat. Her back arched up each time his tongue found her clit.

Her legs trembled and she humped her ass up at him to meet his sucking mouth. A wail of pleasure came out of her throat when his finger touched her asshole.

He looked up at her and grinned. "You like it in the ass?"

"Fuck my pussy!" she moaned. "But do it from behind!"

She watched him strip his clothes off. She knelt on the edge of the bat with her head down and her ass in the air. Reaching back with her hands, she pulled open her ass-cheeks in invitation. He gave a low whistle of appreciation.

"You've got a gorgeous ass!" he said, "How come your husband doesn't take care of you?"

She groaned. "How do you know I'm married?"

"You're wearing a ring," he laughed.

Now she felt his swollen cock-head probing between her wet cunt-lips. She squirmed and wriggled her ass back, trying to capture him. He teased her awhile by rubbing his cock-head over the mouth of her cunt-hole.

Then he finally shoved forward to drill the length of his throbbing cock inside her hot clutching fuck-channel.

He was an expert. If there was anything he didn't know about fucking, she couldn't imagine what it was. Within moments he had her in a delirium, moaning and quaking with pleasure.

His fingertip tickled her ass again, and this time he pushed his finger inside to ream out her shit-tube.

"Oh, God, I'm coming soon! Oh, sweet Jesus, don't stop! Please, don't stop!"

He kept his cock stroking in and out, long smooth strokes that rattled her bones.

"Oh! Oh! Oh! Uunnaggghhh! Oh, God! I'm coming!"

It seemed endless. She came again and again. "Keep fucking me!" she sobbed. "Don't stop fucking me!"

How wet she was! A flood of cunt juice had gushed out of her pussy to wash over her thighs and soak the bed. His balls slapped loudly against her wet ass with each stroke of his plunging fuck-meat.

She mewled and crooned in wanton abandon. It was perfect! It was the perfect fuck! She knew nothing about him except his name, yet there he was behind her drilling big fat cock in and out of her fuck-hole like a well-oiled fucking machine.

He kept fucking her and fucking her. She imagined his cock getting bigger and bigger, stretching the mouth of her cunt-hole more and more as he pumped.

He wiggled her ass, encouraging him. "Fuck me! Fuck me, you sonofabitch! Give it to me!"

He began speeding up his strokes now, and she realized he was about to come. She wanted it. She wanted his hot cream squirting into the channel of her cunt.

His hands clutching her hips, he fucked in and out forcefully.

"Christ, what a beautiful fuck!" he groaned. "You've got a gorgeous big ass!"

He suddenly began spurting his jism, grunting in rhythm with his spurts. She thrust her ass back at him, fucking back at his cock, sucking up his cream with her hungry cunt.

How marvellous it was! She had a cunt full of quivering, erupting cock. It was lovely!

When he finally pulled his dripping prick out of her cunt-hole, she was totally exhausted. She rolled over and shook, her thighs closing tightly to squeeze her completely satisfied, warm, oozing cunt.

CHAPTER NINE

Jeanette visited Kate Dunmore the next day. This time the milkman was nowhere in sight.

Jeanette found it difficult to talk about her troubles with Warren, but Kate was clever enough to finally drag the whole story out of her.

"People don't like to talk about these things," Kate said with a smile.

Jeanette nodded. "Yes, I guess so."

"I have a confession of my own, dear."

"You do?"

"I know you saw me and the milkman yesterday."

Jeanette blushed. "Oh, God!"

Kate patted Jeanette's arm and chuckled. "Don't be upset, dear. I don't mind. His name is Bob and my husband knows all about it. It's one of our little secrets. Did you see everything?"

"Yes," Jeanette whispered. She was dumbfounded. Kate was turning out to be something quite unexpected!

"Bob is a very competent fucker, isn't he?" Kate smiled. There was a faint flush on her milk-white cheeks, not of embarrassment, but as if she were remembering her last session with the milkman. Then she dropped a bombshell.

"You can share him, if you like."

Jeanette stared at her. "Share him?"

"Yes, dear. Now let's have some lunch and I'll tell you what I have in mind."

What Kate had in mind was a threesome, and then maybe something more than that when Kate's husband returned home from his convention.

"It's better to do these things with people you know," Kate said.

Jeanette agreed. Picking up strange studs was dangerous. Harry Baker was a pain in the neck and Phil Avramidis was a selfish slob.

She was also excited by the idea of fucking together with sweet Kate Dunmore. She remembered Julia Baker. It could be fun! Jeanette had a momentary fantasy of sucking on Kate's hairless quim but quickly set it aside.

Two days later, Jeanette found herself sitting in the Dunmore's living room. Once again, Kate was a grass widow, but Bob the milkman turned out to be an easygoing guy with an endless supply of jokes that he told so disarmingly badly that the two women couldn't help laughing.

Jeanette found herself jealous of Kate's contentment. The woman seemed so at ease with herself! Jeanette's pulse raced as she watched Kate taking Bob's hard cock out of his pants. First she pumped her hand up and down on his long thick prick. Then she leaned over to place her mouth directly above his crotch.

Grasping his cock-shaft in one hand, she placed her mouth over his fat red knob and with a quick motion slid her mouth up and down on his cock-shaft two or three times.

Jeanette thought it was much more exciting than watching Harry and Julia Baker. She'd always thought Kate Dunmore was so sweet and innocent. Kate had always reminded Jeanette of a nun and now here was Kate leaning over to suck the cock of the milkman!

Abruptly pulling her mouth away, Kate said, "Let's get all our clothes off!"

Jeanette watched the others as she stripped. She felt strange removing her clothes in front of Kate and Bob, but at the same time it was terribly exciting.

Her eyes feasted on Bob's big cock and bloated balls. He was hairy. For some reason, she'd always found hairiness sexy. She quivered with lust.

Kate's heavy tits were luscious. Her wide pink nipples reminded Jeanette of ripe strawberries. The most interesting thing of all, of course, was Kate's hairless cunt!

Kate also had a nicely shaped ass. Jeanette hadn't seen too much of her ass the last time, because Kate had been stretched out on the kitchen table. No doubt about it, her sweet neighbour was in great shape for a thirty-five year-old!

"I know you've seen this before," Kate chuckled, her hand rubbing her hairless cunt mound. "Were you surprised?"

Jeanette nodded. "It's cute!"

"Bob loves it," Kate said. "Don't you, Bob?"

Chuckling, Bob extended his tongue and swiped it over his lips.

God, my pussy is so wet! Jeanette thought. She wondered if they could smell her arousal.

They all sat down again, and in a moment Kate's mouth was once more moving up and down on Bob's cock. Saliva drooled out of her mouth and down over his cock-shaft and balls.

"She's a great cocksucker," Bob said.

Kate mewled and tickled his balls. Jeanette watched with amazement as Kate's head bobbed deep into his crotch to take Bob's cock far down into her throat.

She was conscious of Bob's eyes on her cunt. Blushing, Jeanette opened her legs to show him her pussy.

"That's the way!" he said.

Sliding both hands down over her belly, she fingered her cunt lips open.

"Oh, Christ, what a cunt!" Bob laughed. Jeanette loved the attention. Kate was on her knees now, her head down over Bob's crotch as she continued sucking him.

Unable to resist the impulse, Jeanette got down behind Kate and ran her hands over Kate's full, rounded ass-cheeks. She fondled her neighbour's hanging tits and then slipped her fingers between the older woman's thighs to finger her bald cunt-lips.

Then she trailed her fingers up the crack of Kate's ass and tickled Kate's asshole. Kate wiggled her hips to show Jeanette she liked what she was doing. How strange it was to touch another woman!

Once more she probed Kate's cunt. This time she pushed her fingers inside. Kate's cunt-meat was hot and wet. Using two fingers, Jeanette began finger-fucking Kate as Kate continued sucking Bob.

Kate finally pulled her mouth off Bob's cock. "I need fucking!" she said huskily. Scrambling to change her position, Kate straddled Bob. She fisted his cock-shaft, pulling it up and down, and then she positioned his cock-head at the mouth of her cunt-hole. She groaned as she eased dawn to impale herself on his rampant fuck-tube.

"Oh, Lord, now that's heavenly!" she moaned.

Jeanette moved behind Kate, putting her arms around her, lifting Kate's heavy tits in her hands. She marvelled at Kate's lust. The older woman was so different than the woman she'd thought she knew!

She wondered about Henry Dunmore. She wondered what it would be like to fuck him.

Tweaking Kate's nipples, she pressed her cunt bush against Kate's back.

Kate giggled. "I can never came this way, but I love it!" Soon she slipped off Bob's cock. "Take me from behind!" she said, her voice full of urgency.

Bob's cock was pink and angry-looking; Jeanette could see a long strand of clear fuck juice hanging from its tip. He got up, one hand holding his balls. Kate kneeled on a big hassock, leaning forward to rest her head on her arms. Her ass was up in the air, big and inviting.

Bob moved behind Kate now. Putting his hands on her ass, he squeezed her flesh, his cock swaying back and forth, his cock-head still dripping juice. Leaning forward, he fingered Kate's tits, teasing the large pink nubs.

Then he fisted his cock and swabbed it up and down between her cunt and her asshole. His fat fuck-pole probed between Kate's cunt-lips. At last he found her fuck-hole. He pushed forward with a grunt and plunged his cock into the hilt with one slippery stroke.

Jeanette moved behind him. Running one hand over his ass, she grabbed his balls with her other hand. She gently squeezed and palpated his large nuts, pulling on his ball-bag as he began pumping his fuck-meat in and out of Kate's cunt.

Jeanette's thumb found Bob's asshole and she massaged the slightly raised grommet and finally pushed inside.

"Oh, fuck!" he groaned.

Impaled on his cock, Kate squirmed her ass back at him. "Oh, Jesus, fuck me hard!"

Bob grunted as he pumped his cock in and out of her juicy fuck-channel.

Jeanette fingered her cunt with her free hand. Wild with need, she pushed two fingers inside her cunt-hole and rapidly pumped them in and out.

"Oh, God, what a cock!" Kate groaned. "Keep fucking me! Don't stop!"

Bob gasped. Jeanette felt his balls jump in her hand. He suddenly cried out and began driving his cock with piston-like strokes in and out of Kate's hungry pussy.

"Oh, fuck, I'm coming!" he rasped.

His balls jerked and started to retract as he began shooting his load. Jeanette loved the feel of his nuts – the size of walnuts, she guessed. She shivered, her hand clutching his scrotal sac, as he filled Kate's cunt with his hot cock-cream.

When he finally pulled his cock out of Kate's cunt, she turned over on the hassock with her legs spread wide. Jeanette could see Bob's pearly jism oozing out of her neighbour's angry pink pussy.

With a soft moan, Jeanette knelt down between Kate's legs and plastered her mouth against Kate's wet cunt. She sucked and licked, lapping up Bob's thick cream, sucking Kate's petal-like cunt-lips until the lovely golden-haired woman moaned with delight. The combined flavours of cock- and cunt-cream were like nothing she'd ever experienced before. She had reached cloud nine.

At last she pulled her mouth away from Kate's juice-drenched cunt and finger fucked herself furiously until she came with a deep guttural wail.

Afterwards Jeanette sucked Bob's cock to get him hard again. Her lips formed in a tight oval, she bobbed her head up and down, sucking at his prick. It wasn't long before his cock began to thicken. She could feel his cock-meat throbbing in her mouth.

Kate helped by holding his balls while Jeanette

slurped steadily on his hardening cock. Soon his fuck-pole was back in working order again. Then she eased back, sucking only his cock-head. Saliva ran down from her lips and over Kate's hand. Bob had the women sit on either side of him. He played with their tits while they worked on his cock and bills. His fingers wandered down to Jeanette's pussy. She opened her legs and he was soon probing between her cunt-lips, shoving two fingers into her cunt-hole, pumping them in and out.

Kate slipped off the sofa. Jeanette gasped when she felt Kate's head burrowing between her thighs. She pulled one leg up, exposing her crotch, and soon Kate had her mouth attached to Jeanette's wet cunt.

Kate sucked gluttonously at Jeanette's brimming vulva and then moved up to massage Jeanette's clit with her tongue. The trio finally broke apart.

"I want to watch him fuck you again," Jeanette said.

Kate laughed. "I should think you'd want some of it yourself, dear."

"Not yet. Let me watch you again."

This time Kate lay down on the rug with her legs pulled up. Jeanette sat back and fingered her cunt slowly as she watched Bob mount Kate. He draped Kate's legs over his shoulders. He pushed forward and rammed his cock deep into her bald cunt.

Kneeling down beside the couple on the floor, Jeanette bent forward to get a close look. She was excited at the sight of his cock slapping in and out of her friend's dripping pussy!

She ran her hands over Kate's ass and finally moved her fingers into the junction of cock and cunt. Kate's cunt juice streamed over Jeanette's fingers. Jeanette rubbed Bob's pumping cock-shaft as it plunged in and out of her neighbour's vagina.

Pulling her hand away, Jeanette lowered her head and managed to get her mouth fastened half on Kate's cunt and half on Bob's ramming prick. She sucked and licked the hot fuck-meat. The lewdness of what she was doing made her tremble. How thrilling it was to have Bob's cock sliding back and forth past her lips as he fucked Kate.

When she finally removed her mouth from the wet slippery junction, she moved up and dropped one of her tits onto Kate's face.

"Oh, yes!" said Kate. Opening her mouth, she began sucking hard on Jeanette's fat nipple. Then she pulled her mouth away and looked at Jeanette.

"Let me have your cunt!" Kate said. "Sit on my face!"

Jeanette thrilled at the lewd command and groaned as she moved to do Kate's bidding. She positioned herself over Kate's face, squatting over her head, and gradually eased down until she had her cunt plastered on Kate's waiting mouth.

"Suck me!" Jeanette shouted. "Suck me out! Suck my pussy!"

She sat down on Kate's face. She began rocking gently up and down, then with more force, grinding her cunt into the woman's upturned face. It was wonderful! She massaged her crotch, rubbed her cunt-hole against Kate's chin, and made her swollen clit quiver against Kate's nose.

Oh, God, I love this! She thought. How delicious it was to have her cunt mashed down on someone's face!

Kate's hands were clutching Jeanette's ass-cheeks, and now Kate pulled Jeanette forward until Jeanette's ass was over Kate's mouth. Jeanette gasped as she felt Kate's tongue tickling her asshole.

A moment later Kate's tongue slithered inside Jeanette's asshole and began fucking in and out. The feel of Kate's wet tongue fucking her little brownie drove Jeanette wild.

"Mmmmmm! Oh, Jesus, that's good!" she crooned. "Oh, God, yes! Oh, God, she's got her tongue up my ass!"

Bob laughed and suddenly pulled his cock out of Kate's cunt. "Come on, Jeanette," he growled. "Let me have some of that hot pussy!"

Trembling, Jeanette fell forward on her hands and knees. Kate quickly got out of the way.

Bob scrambled behind Jeanette, his hands holding her ass, his cock-head bouncing into the crack between her ass-cheeks. A moment later Jeanette groaned as his bloated knob stretched the mouth of her cunt-hole and drilled forward to ream out her fuck-channel.

Squirming on the rug, Kate slipped underneath Jeanette until her face was under the pretty brunette's hanging tits. Jeanette shivered and lowered herself to drop a nipple in Kate's open mouth.

Now Bob was fucking her without mercy, pile-driving his cock in and out of her drenched cunt. Each thrust made her quiver and moan. Her tits wobbled against Kate's face.

Then with a grunt Bob pulled his cock out of Jeanette's cunt-hole and he pressed his cock-head against her tight asshole. She held her breath and now finding it far easier to relax her anal sphincter at short notice, was able to accommodate the milkman's sizeable prick as he pushed forward to ram it deep into her buttery rectal depths.

"Oh, shit, what a hot ass!" he groaned.

He continued to ram his cock home to the hilt up Jeanette's shit-tube. Kate squirmed again under Jeanette's body, this time positioning her face under Jeanette's crotch.

"Uunngghhh!" Jeanette cried, when she felt Kate's mouth on her cunt. She had a man's fat cock up her ass and a woman's soft mouth on her pussy! Throwing her head back, she cried out her lust and convulsed in a shuddering orgasm.

CHAPTER TEN

As the weeks passed, Warren noticed a change in Jeanette, but he had no idea what it was all about. She seemed to be spending a great deal of time with Kate Dunmore. Warren couldn't understand that. Jeanette had always claimed that Kate was sweet but dull. It was difficult to believe that they'd suddenly become friends.

Warren shrugged it off. If Jeanette wanted to be friends with Kate, that was her business.

Henry Dunmore, Kate's husband, always talked a great deal about the Bible, and considering all the time Jeanette was spending at the Dunmore house, Warren worried that one day Jeanette might become some sort of born-again religious nut.

One afternoon when Jeanette was in town, Warren was surprised to receive a call from Kate inviting him over to taste a new apple pie she had just made.

When he arrived at the house, he learned that Henry was away at a church meeting. He and Kate had never been alone like this. She was wearing a skimpy halter and tight shorts, and he couldn't help but notice her big tits and curvy ass. Her hair was down, no longer tied up in its habitual bun, and she wasn't wearing her eyeglasses. He wondered what she was like in bed. Was she as dull as she seemed?

It wasn't long before he realized that she had more in mind than apple pie. She was being deliberately seductive. He was shocked at first but he was also flattered.

His eyes continued raking over her body, and it wasn't long before his cock grew hard inside his pants. Sweet and prudish Kate Dunmore suddenly seemed as sexy as hell!

He imagined himself getting her into bed and fucking her blind. He imagined her fingers under his balls tickling his asshole. He imagined the shaft of his cock sliding between her lush tits. He imagined her tongue licking his cock-head.

Would she suck him off? He thought of his cock sliding in and out of her warm mouth and then pulling away from her lips dripping with her saliva and ready for a good hard fucking.

Kate seemed to recognize the lust in his eyes, and it wasn't long before she was smiling and pressing herself against him.

"I think you're interested in more than my apple pie," she said.

He knew she could feel his hard-on pressing against her belly. He grunted and pushed closer to her, rubbing his cock against her belly.

"Oh, that feels lovely!" she crooned. Then she

looked up at him. "Don't get any wrong ideas about this," she said. "I love my husband, but sometimes it's nice to play with someone else. Are you interested?"

"You can't tell about people," Warren said.

"No you can't!" she laughed. "Jeanette says you're a little shy about sex. Is it true?"

His face reddened. How strange it was that this woman who had always seemed too prudish was questioning him like this.

"Try me," he said gruffly.

Laughing softly, she took him by the hand and led him to the couch. They sat down and she leaned over him. She kissed him, mashing her lips against his, plunging her tongue into his mouth.

His cock throbbed as he began moving his hands over her body. His fingers slipped inside her halter-top and cupped the mound of one tit. He fondled the heavy globe, pinching the berry-like nipple.

"Let's go into the bedroom!" she whispered.

In a daze, he followed her into the bedroom, his eyes fixed on the full mounds of her ass. His cock was as hard as a rock.

Inside the bedroom she turned and came into his arms. Once more their lips fused in a hot kiss. Once more she thrust her hot tongue deep inside his mouth.

He groaned and pressed his body closer to hers. She seemed wild with passion. Her earthy response turned him on. They fell onto the bed, their arms and legs entangled.

"Let's get undressed!" she whispered in his ear. "I'll do you first!"

He stretched out and watched her. She rose up on her knees, leaning over him. His eyes feasted on the swell of her tits. He held back, resisting the urge to suck a pink nipple into his mouth.

She unbuttoned his shirt, peeling it off his shoulders and pulling it away. Bending forward, she licked his chest lightly, nibbling at his nipples with her teeth. He groaned.

"Christ, you're a hot bitch!" he said.

Smiling, she worked on the buckle of his belt. Her fingers moved swiftly and expertly and soon she had his pants and shorts pulled down to his ankles. She slipped them off his feet and pushed them away.

Leaning over him, she cupped his cock in her hand. "My, what a lovely prick!" she said.

The glitter in her eyes drove him crazy. Now she stripped off her halter-top and shorts. Her tits tumbled free. They were like ripe juicy melons, large and heavy.

He gazed at her smooth thighs and then down at her crotch. His eyes widened when he saw her hairless pussy. She giggled and opened her legs to him. He could see the glistening of her juices in her cunt.

"Oh, Jesus," he groaned. "I want to suck that – let me suck your cunt!"

Mewling with approval, she moved forward and straddled his chest. He stared at her gaping pussy, at the pink pulsating meat of her cunt. He could see the thick, flushed outer lips as well as the delicate furling of her inner lips. Between them he observed the little trickles of clear juice oozing out of her quim, her tiny piss hole, the ragged pink flesh that was the entrance to her vagina and further down, the puckering of her neat, nut-brown anus. He could see everything!

His cock hardened and trembled in response.

He pulled at her ass-cheeks, trying to get her cunt over his face. She laughed and pushed her pussy forward.

He lashed out with his tongue, swabbing up and down between her cunt-flaps and lapping over her clit. She pressed down, forcing his nose into her cunt. The gentle, musky fragrance of her pussy intoxicated him.

She held his head gently, rubbing her cunt up and down over his nose and lips, her dripping cunt-hole mashed against his mouth. Then suddenly she pulled away from him.

Turning her body, she straddled him again, this time with her cunt over his face and her mouth over his cock. Her thighs were spread wide. Her fingers took hold of his cock and began pumping his cock-skin up and down.

She lowered her wet pussy mound to his face. He opened his mouth wide, his tongue fluttering. When her cunt mashed down against his mouth, he began sucking.

He pulled and chewed at her cunt-lips. He flicked his tongue back and forth over the knob of her clit.

"Yes! Yes!" she cried, "Oooohhh! Yes! Yes!"

She wiggled her ass over his face, bearing down hard, rubbing back and forth to increase the friction of his sucking.

Her hand pumped his cock. He bucked his ass up. He wanted her mouth on his cock. He wanted the feel of her lips moving up and down his cock-shaft.

His mouth filled with cunt, he groaned and pressed his cock up at her head.

Now Kate gasped. "Please suck me!" she begged. "Suck me harder! I'll get to your cock in a minute, but now, please, just suck me!"

His cheeks and chin dripped with her hot cunt juice. He thrust his tongue in and out of her cunt-hole faster and harder. The muscles of her fuck-channel grabbed at his tongue, squeezing it, pulling at it. His nose nestled in the crevice of her buttocks, pressed hard against her brown anus.

His hands probed the cheeks of her ass, pinching and fondling her plump flesh. His tongue swapped up and down the crack between her cunt-hole and right up to her asshole.

He wondered why he and Jeanette never did things like this. It seemed crazy that here he was with their next-door neighbour doing all the things he wanted to do with his wife.

Now Kate convulsed in a religious orgasm. "Oooooohhh!" she wailed. "Oh, sweet Lord!" He felt her cunt muscles contract around his tongue.

After a moment Kate lowered her face. He could feel her hot breath against his cock. Then suddenly she clamped her mouth over his cock-head and he gasped at the warm pussy-like feeling of her mouth.

Holding his cock-shaft in her hand, she licked her tongue all over his velvety knob. She made a tight ring of her lips to massage his cock as she moved her mouth up and down over his throbbing fuck-pole.

Her hand slowly pumped his cock-shaft while she sucked. Her tits hung heavily on his belly. Wriggling her ass, she clamped her thighs around his head till he could no longer hear the sinking sounds she made as she slobbered over his meat.

He felt her lips nibbling on his cock-flesh. He felt his cock-head rubbing against the back of her throat. Then her throat suddenly seemed to open and his cock shot forward even deeper until her throat muscles clutched his cock-head.

His ass backed up off the bed at the incredible pleasure of her sucking. Her fingers tickled up and down the sensitive stretch of skin between his balls and his asshole.

He had his cock in her throat! The tightness of it blew his mind. She sucked and pulled on his cock in a way he had never experienced before.

He sensed that she wanted his load down her throat. Pulling his mouth any from her cunt for just a moment, he cried out, "Aw, shit, fucking hell!"

She pushed her pussy down again on his open mouth. Then she shifted forward until he found his lips covering her asshole and his chin digging into her cunt, crazy with lust, he stiffened his tongue and pushed it into the tight ring of her brownie.

A moment later he could feel her finger working around his own asshole and finally pushing in to ream out his shit-tube.

Christ, what a slut! He thought. What a fucking hot bitch!

Working his hand under his chin, he squeezed his thumb into her hot cunt-hole. She was bobbing her head up and down on his cock now, fucking him with her mouth, sucking his cock-meat to the same tempo as the grinding of her hips against his face.

A flood of cunt juice squirted out of her cunt-hole to stream over his face and hand. Her asshole quivered and sucked around the root of his tongue. He felt her shuddering, and then suddenly spasm after spasm wracked her body.

He bucked upward, his balls rattling, his jism

blasting hotly out of the tip of his cock. He pumped seven or eight spurts of his hot cream against the back of her throat.

She sucked and drank, her tongue fluttering over his cock-head as she drained the load out of his balls. She carefully licked up every drop. They finally rolled apart, gasping. "Oh, Jesus!" he croaked.

Kate bent over him and laughed softly. "Your face is all wet with my cunt juice," she teased. "What would you like to do next?"

"Good grief, woman!" he rasped. "I'm not ready yet."

"You will be!" she smiled. "Don't worry about that. What would you like?"

"Do you like it in your ass?"

"I like it anywhere," she replied. "I'd love that! Does Jeanette like it in her ass?"

"We don't do very much in bed," he said. She smirked. The look in her eyes told him that she knew more about his married life than he'd realized.

"Why not?" she said. "Maybe you ought to try. You might be surprised at Jeanette."

He wondered how much she knew. She was right, of course. He really ought to try.

"What I need now is a good long fuck!" she said. "I want that gorgeous cock in my cunt!"

Rolling over onto her back, she pulled her knees up and spread them wide apart. He sat up and looked down at her. His eyes feasted on her wet, pink maw of her insatiable cunt.

She squirmed her ass on the mattress, taunting him with her juicy pussy. Then her hands moved down and she pulled her cunt-lips open with her fingers.

He stared at the gaping hole, at the pink meat coated with cunt-juice. His cock was growing again. She looked down at it and laughed.

"My cunt is turning you on, so come on, honey!" she crooned, and held her arms out to him. "You can have my ass later. Right now I want my cunt reamed out. I want that big cock in there." Moving into her arms, he fit himself into the saddle between her thighs.

"Slip it to me!" she gasped.

She gripped his cock in her hand and guided his cock-head to the mouth of her cunt-hole. His fuck-pole slid smoothly into the slippery wet swamp of her cunt.

She moaned at the first thrust. She raised her hips off the bed to take as much of his cock as possible. Grunting with excitement, he stuffed his throbbing cock-meat into her soft fuck-tube.

God, how wet she was! She pulled her legs up, and began rocking them back and forth with a slow motion that drove his cock in and out of her pussy.

"Oh, yeah!" he breathed. "That's good! Keep that up!"

"Fuck me!" she groaned. "Give it to me!"

He could feel her cunt muscles clasping his cock, sucking inward, trying to pull him into her body.

"Oh, Christ!" he croaked.

"Now don't blaspheme, honey," she giggled. "Do you like that?"

"It's marvellous!" he gasped.

Her cunt was a wide-open, hungry hole trying to swallow him up. She twisted her ass, churning her cunt on his cock, pumping her pussy up and down on the slab of fuck-meat, stretching the mouth of her cunt-hole.

"I'm fucking you!" she laughed. "Are you going to come soon?"

"Almost!" he rasped.

"Let it come!" she crooned. "Squirt your jism! Shoot it, baby, shoot it!"

Her feet flew up and down, her heels slapping into the crack of his ass. Her cunt sucked at his cock. Her hips gyrated and twisted as she squirmed the meat of her pussy on his fuck-pole.

He could hear the slurping noise made by his cock as he thrust it in and out of her slippery pussy. He pounded up and down against her crotch, driving his cock all the way in and then pulling it out again until he had only his cock-head inside the mouth of her cunt.

His shaft mashed against her clit. She groaned with pleasure at the end of each stroke, her heavy tits jiggling as his balls slapped against her ass.

"Fuck me, lover!" she cried, bouncing her ass up and down. "Fuck me good!"

She mewled in rhythm to his bucking hips, tossing her head from side to side, moaning, urging him on. He thrilled at her response. He and Jeanette had never yet had a wild fuck like this.

"Fuck me, honey! I'm coming!" she cried out.

A wild yelp came out of her throat as he began ramming his cock in and out of her cunt. Her ass shook and quivered. His cock bucked up at her faster and faster and then his jism was spurting again, filling her cunt-channel, gushing out of his cock-head to splash against the clutching walls of her pussy.

He pumped and groaned. He held her ass in his hands. His cock jerked and twitched. Her thighs clasped around his waist. Her tits felt hot against his chest.

He had never fucked like this before, not with anyone!

"Oh, Jeez... I mean... aw shit!" he gasped.

She arched up against him, pumping back at his cock, trying to wring the last of his load out of his balls.

As he slumped down, he heard a feminine gasp behind him and then a man's voice.

"Well, well," a deep, slow male voice said. "Now just what the *hell's* going on here?"

His heart caught in his throat, Warren turned and looked behind him. Jeanette was standing beside the tall figure of Henry Dunmore. She giggled.

"I think they're fucking," she said.

CHAPTER ELEVEN

The first time someone suggested they tie her up, Jeanette resisted the idea and then finally yielded.

A month had passed since Jeanette and Henry had walked in on Warren and Kate. Kate had planned the whole thing. Warren was a bit angry at first, but he soon calmed down.

He was excited by Jeanette's new sexuality. He quickly learned to relax his inhibitions with her. After that it was only natural that the Townsends and Dunmores get together frequently for evenings of fucking.

It was obvious to Jeanette that Warren and Kate really turned each other on. She didn't care. Things were so crazy now! There were even times when Bob the milkman joined their orgies.

Now they wanted to tie her up!

"I think you'll like it!" Kate whispered.

Jeanette shivered. The idea of being tied up and helpless while they worked her body over made her legs tremble and her pussy gush cunt juice.

They decided the Dunmore's four-poster bed was ideal. They made Jeanette remove her blouse. They tied her wrists to the bedposts.

Henry laughed as he ran his fingers over her ribs. She shivered as she imagined the lewd picture she made. She felt helpless. Her tits bulged out of her bra.

In a way she was frightened. They could do anything they wanted to her, and there would be no way for her to resist. They would be able to tease her until they drove her wild.

Henry had his hands on her tits now. He squeezed each globe lightly, now and then his fingers pressing into her flesh. He kneaded her tits as if they were two mounds of dough.

Warren knelt beside her, his hands stroking her under her skirt. He lightly fondled her ass and her clit. Her body spasmed at the tantalizing touch of his fingers.

Kate climbed onto the bed. She unbuttoned her blouse, slipped it off, and tossed it away. Her heavy tits, with their wide pink caps, shook as she removed her bra and tossed it aside as well.

She pulled on her nipples, rolling them between her fingers. Then she shifted forward on her knees and leaned against Jeanette's back.

"How are you doing, honey?" she smiled.

She unhooked Jeanette's bra so that Henry could get his hands on her bare tits. He leaned forward to kiss and suck her nipples. Jeanette gasped at the feel of his wet mouth on the sensitive buds.

Kate's hands joined her husband's on Jeanette's heaving moist-tipped globes. Four sets of fingers mauled and squeezed her trembling flesh. She moaned and whimpered with the pleasure of it.

Henry finally pulled away with an deep, throaty laugh.

"Play with her while I get my clothes off," he said to his wife.

Jeanette watched him strip away his clothes. She was eager for fucking now. How wicked it was! She breathed heavily as she watched Henry tear off his clothes.

The first time she'd fucked Henry, he'd turned out to be a complete surprise. He was lusty, even more than Kate. His obsession with religion didn't seem to interfere with his craving for fucking.

Henry said God gave people cunts and cocks to use them. Now his cock was jutting upward, his circumcised cock-head glistening, his piss-hole brimming with juice.

A network of prominent blue veins covered his thick cock-shaft. His ball-bag hung down like a leather pouch from the base of his cock. She could see the outline of his huge, low-hanging nuts.

Jeanette's cunt tingled with hunger. Her knees trembled, cunt juice running down her thighs. She wiggled and squirmed with pleasure and anticipation.

Now Warren probed his fingers between her cunt-lips. Kate's hands were on Jeanette's tits and she massaged them slowly, teasing Jeanette's nipples with her fingertips and nails.

Jeanette pressed back against Kate's body, excited by the feel of Kate's tits against her skin. She rubbed herself against her friend's nipples.

She loved the erotic contact with another

woman. She'd been surprised at how stimulating it could be.

Warren ran his hands up and down her thighs. He rubbed her cunt juice up and down the insides of her firm white thighs. He squeezed and kneaded her ass-cheeks. His fingers dipped into the heat of her cunt.

"Mmmmmmm!" Jeanette moaned. She pushed her crotch forward, asking for more.

The sensations produced by all the hands working on her body overwhelmed her. Moans of pleasure escaped her lips. Head tossing, hair flying, her breath came in gasps.

Laughing, Kate whispered in her ear. "It works, doesn't it, honey?"

Jeanette's response was another moan. Henry was unzipping her skirt now. He stripped off her skirt and panties and pulled them down and off, tossing them away.

She looked at Warren. He had his clothes off. His cock seemed bigger and heavier than ever before. He was obviously turned on by having sex tied up like this. She could see the excitement in his eyes.

As if in a dream, she watched Warren and Kate come together on the bed. Kate clasped Warren's hips between her thighs.

Jeanette clamped her own thighs together as Henry ran his fingers through her pubic bush. Then she spread her legs apart.

"That's the way, baby!" Henry laughed.

Before she realized what he was doing, she found her legs tied to the bed. She was spread open wide. She could feel the coolness on her cunt. Her pussy gaped hungrily.

His eyes glittering, Henry stood back and

looked her up and down. He reached down and squeezed her tits. He stroked her belly. His fingers continued to toy with her cunt-hair.

Then he ran both hands into her pussy. He held her cunt-lips between his thumbs and forefingers and pulled them apart. He stretched and tugged her thick pussy-lips until she moaned.

Now he slipped his finger inside her cunt hole, probing at her fuck-channel.

"Oh, Jesus!" she moaned.

Her hips pumped back and forth as she attempted to fuck his hand.

Once again Kate moved under Jeanette. Her thighs wide apart, she snuggled her pussy against Jeanette's ass and pressed her tits flat against Jeanette's back. Her arms encircled Jeanette's waist. She held Jeanette immobilized as Henry knelt down and pressed his mouth into Jeanette's cunt.

"Uunnggghhh!" Jeanette shuddered and bucked her ass up to Henry's fluttering tongue.

Henry was an expert cunt-sucker. He thrust his tongue in and out of her steaming fuck-hole and then moved it up to tease her clit. He licked up and down, swabbing the thick tip of his tongue over her quivering little button.

"Oh! Ooooohhh!" she moaned. "Oh, my God…"

She wailed. She twisted with pleasure. Kate continued pressing her pubic mound against Jeanette's ass and playing with Jeanette's tits. Cunt juice gushed out of Jeanette's pussy to soak the insides of her thighs. She was hot! They were turning her into an animal!

She pumped her hips back and forth frantically, pressing her ass against Kate's belly and pushing her pussy against Henry's probing tongue.

Her face contorted with lust, her forehead beaded with sweat, she wailed and moaned with excitement. She was sandwiched between husband and wife. How glorious it was!

Now Henry's tongue forced back the quivering hood of her clit. He closed his mouth over the tiny knob and began to suck.

"Oh, dear God!" Jeanette whimpered. "Make me come! Please, make me come!"

Henry sucked steadily. Warren was standing nearby, watching as Henry sucked at his wife's pussy. Jeanette quivered and trembled at the craziness of it, at the freaky way in which her husband was watching two other people work her over.

Then Warren crawled on the bed and manoeuvred himself behind Kate. His hands slipped under Kate's ass to fondle her cunt. Kate squealed and wriggled her crotch on Warren's fingers.

He pushed three fingers into Kate's cunt and with a rapid movement pumped them in and out.

"Oh, you fucker!" Kate said. "That's good!"

She reached back to catch his cock in her fist. Her hand pumped up and down on his cock-shaft. Jeanette turned her head and caught the motion of Kate's hand on her husband's cock. She groaned. How exciting it was to watch another woman fondle her husband's prick!

She pumped her crotch, snapping Henry's head back and forth. Henry finally looked up at her and grinned.

"You're really getting into it aren't you, baby?"

"Oh, God!" Jeanette wailed. "I want somebody to fuck me!"

Henry rose up now. His cock pushed into her

belly. She gazed down at his bloated cock-head, brimming with clear pre-cum. She gyrated her hips, grinding her belly on his pulsating fuck-meat. Snickering, Henry bent down now to untie her ankles. His hands moved around to clutch her ass-cheeks. He pulled her forward. She raised up her knees and wrapped her legs around his hips.

She squirmed as he positioned his cock-head at the mouth of her cunt. A moment later he plunged his cock into the hilt, ramming her cunt with his hard fuck-pole until her cunt-lips were jammed up against the base of his prick and she could feel his rubbery cock head bump against her cervix.

He stroked in and out with rapid-fire strokes. Her tits bounced and swayed. She opened her mouth and groaned at the pleasure of his hard fucking.

She squirmed as he slammed against her pussy. A wail came out of her throat as he ploughed his hard cock in and out of her wet fuck-channel.

Warren was on his back now. Kate was straddling him, her fuck-hole sliding up and down on his cock. She bounced her ass and giggled, swallowing up his cock to the balls and then pulling up to his cock-head.

Her clutching fuck-channel moved up and down the length of his wet fuck-meat. Her tits jiggled and swayed. Loud grunts came out of her throat. Each time she came down, Warren's hips surged up to meet her downward stroke.

His knees rocked from side to side as he pumped his cock up and down on her clutching cunt. Her meaty ass squirmed as she ground down on his crotch. Her ass-cheeks quivered as the walls of her fuck-channel clutched and relaxed in frequent spasms.

At last Henry pulled his cock out of Jeanette's cunt and they untied her. She wanted more fucking.

"Oh, God. Fuck me again!" she cried.

Henry chuckled and pushed her back on the bed. Lifting up her thighs, he draped her legs over his shoulders and sank his cock deep into her pussy.

"Juicy little pussy!" he said out loud, but as if to himself.

He stroked his cock in and out a few times and then he pulled out. Warren replaced him. She groaned when she realized her husband was fucking her.

"Your cunt feels good!" Warren grunted. "You turn me on more than ever."

Jeanette shivered. Turning her head, she watched Henry fucking Kate. The two women lay side by side on the bed, their legs draped over the shoulders of their husbands, their asses bucking upwards as the cocks pistonned in and out of their wet cunts.

As if on signal, the men pulled their cocks out of the dripping pussies and ordered the women to suck them.

Hurrying to obey, the two wives sat up and capped their mouths over the rampant cock-heads. Warren's bloated knob throbbed in Jeanette's mouth. She sucked and slurped on his cock-meat.

Then they switched partners and Jeanette found herself sucking her lips up and down on Henry's thick cock-shaft. The frantic face fucking drove her wild.

Pulling her mouth off Henry's cock, Jeanette groaned and scrambled of the bed to kneel on the floor on all fours. A cackle came out of Henry's throat as he crouched down to kneel behind her.

"My ass!" Jeanette moaned. "Stick it up my ass! Loosen it with your fingers first!"

His lust-crazed eyes gazing down at the deep crack of her ass, Henry scooped some cunt juice out of her pussy and swabbed it over the tight ring of her asshole.

Kate was not to be outdone. In a moment she was kneeling on the floor beside Jeanette. Warren moved down behind her and swabbed his cock into the crack of her ass.

Henry was pushing his cock-head against Jeanette's asshole now, and a moment later his fat knob popped into the elastic ring.

All the ass-fucking Jeanette had experienced during the past months had widened her asshole. Henry's cock entered her shit-tube with ease.

She mewled with joy. "Oh! Oh! *Ohhhhh!*" she crooned.

She squealed and hissed as each inch of his cock advanced into the hot grip of her shitter. She could feel the throbbing of his cock in the channel of her shit-tube.

Henry grunted, pumping his meat in and out with long smooth strokes. He started coming.

"Uunnnggghhh!" Henry grunted.

Jeanette's tummy contracted violently as his hot cream splashed into her bowels. She gasped for breath as if she had been winded while he pumped in and out of her bung. Her face was a mask, contorted with lustful pleasures.

Looking over at Kate and her husband, she watched Warren pumping his hips as he drove his cock in and out of Kate's brown grommet. She looked at Kate's face. Their eyes met. They

smiled at each other.

Warren suddenly grunted and stiffened. He cried out as he began shooting his load into Kate's rubbery shit-tube.

Afterward they made a daisy-chain. They fell down together on the bed. Not really caring where it had just been, Jeanette gave Warren's cock a quick wipe and then was in her mouth while Henry sucked her pussy. Kate sucked Henry's cock while Warren licked Kate's cunt.

They sucked and slurped and slobbered over each other's crotches until the four of them began twitching and jerking together in their various stages of climax.

Later that evening, when Jeanette and Warren were back in their own bedroom, Jeanette asked Warren if he still loved her.

A smouldering look came into his eyes. "Like I said already today. More than I ever did."

He was lying in bed. She came over to him. Looking down at him, she slipped a hand below her belly and massaged the lips of her pussy. His eyes were glued to the movements of her fingers.

She probed into her cunt-hole, pumping her finger in and out, and then pulled it out glistening wet with her cunt juice.

Warren fondled his limp cock. "Get it hard for me," he said.

Jeanette smiled with contentment. There was nothing more delicious than a nightcap fuck after a wild evening with the Dunmores.

She climbed onto the bed and knelt over Warren's crotch. Her fingers curled gently around his soft cock. She rubbed his pink cock-head against the lips of her cunt.

His cock was soon hard enough, his cock-head engorged and glistening wetly with her cunt juice.

Bending down, she closed her lips over his hot knob. She slowly slipped the ring of her lips down his cock-shaft until she had his cock-head jabbing at the back of her throat.

The feel of his throbbing cock-meat stuffing her mouth was utterly thrilling. It almost made her come. She sucked on him, gluttonously slurping.

"Christ, you really know how to suck a cock!" he said.

He held her head in place, and began pumping his hips to work his cock in and out of her mouth. Finally she pulled her mouth off his cock and rolled onto her back.

Lifting her knees, she hooked her forearms behind them and pulled her legs back. Her pink cunt gaped at him in lewd welcome.

With a smile, he positioned himself between her legs, gazing down at her with unmistakable adoration in his eyes.

"You're ready for a hot fuck, you little nympho bitch, aren't you?" he said, grinning.

"Oh, yes!" she said, her voice low and shaking with lust. "Give it to me!" Fisting his cock-shaft, he probed his cock between her inner labia until he found her entrance to her vagina. A moment later he lurched forward to drive his hard, fleshy pole deep inside her.

"Oh, God, yes!" Jeanette cried. "Fuck me! I love it! I may be a little nympho bitch, but I'll always be *your* nympho bitch!"

Her hips bucked up, and she was soon writhing against him, holding her legs high and gripping her knees. Her ass gyrated in circular motions as she fucked back at his cock.

His balls slapped heavily at her asshole with each stroke.

"Fuck me!" she moaned. "Fuck me hard!"

He grinned as he pounded her pussy. His cock stroked in and out, his thick cock-shaft slurping in the juice drenching her cunt. Her body trembled with each forceful thrust of his rampant flesh. A cry came out of her throat each time his turgid, rubbery glans jabbed at the end of her fuck-channel.

"Oh, God, give it to me!" she crooned. "Fuck me good, honey!"

He grinned. Whatever troubles they had had in the past no longer mattered. They were as one now. Her cunt was stuffed and rammed by his cock and the future would bring them nothing but happiness. All the fucking she had done had served only to bring them closer together. Groaning once more, she rammed her finger up his ass as he began shooting his load of hot jism into her quivering cunt. She came with her vagina going into spasm as it received spurt after spurt of his thick, creamy spunk.

THE END

Review Subscriber

JESSICA RODER

THROUGH A GLASS DARKLY...
A PHOTOGRAPHIC JOURNEY
OF SEXUAL DISCOVERY

THE BANKER'S WIFE
John Barbour

Funny how an innocent encounter can turn people's lives upside-down. When Harry and Diane Laurence 'clicked' with Max and Penny Byron at the year's dullest cocktail party, it might have gone no further than improving a potentially ghastly evening for these attractive couples. But the sexually sophisticated Byrons like to swing, and once they'd targeted the innocent young Laurences, the banker and his wife won't rest until they've scored – big time. Moreover, the banker's bisexual wife wants to play with both husband *and* wife. Penny is a beautiful, dangerous woman, just as predatory as her affluent, randy husband, while Diane Laurence's almost virginal naiveté and her husband's lack of experience leaves her totally exposed to this older couple's fiendish machinations.

Orderline: 0800 026 25 24
Email: eps@leadline.co.uk
Post: EPS, 54 New Street, Worcester WR1 2DL

ERB

WWW.EROTICPRINTS.ORG

THE RAVISHED AMERICAN BRIDE

Bob Stainer

When Edward Tremayne brings Molly, his pretty new American bride, back to Cornwall, he warns her that his folks are not quite like others. Indeed, she is not expecting Firethorn, a large, imposing period house crammed to the eves with her delightful adult in-laws. Young Molly soon falls victim to the charm of her handsome father-in-law Piers, and his wife, Georgina, who looks almost the same age as their teenage children. But on the very first night of her stay she discovers a family secret that pulls her down into a spiral of decadent lust and depravity...

With oral, anal, and lesbian action, group incest, orgies and non-stop sex, this is a superb erotic tale in the setting of the lush English countryside. With superb illustrations by Tom Sargent.

Orderline: 0800 026 25 24
Email: eps@leadline.co.uk
Post: EPS, 54 New Street, Worcester WR1 2DL

WWW.EROTICPRINTS.ORG

ACADEMY
OF
LUST

Jenny Strong

Emily and Olivia Newbridge are heirs to a fabulously wealthy business empire that, one day, 22-year-old Emily is determined to run. Both sisters lack social skills, so their guardians send 18-year-old Olivia to a Swiss finishing school while Emily's employers invite her to a weekend seminar. Shockingly, both sisters are subjected to every sadistic torment and humiliation in the book! In their separate punishment worlds, they are forced to experience corporal punishment, public defloration, and many appalling perversions. But their bondage hells become submissive heavens and they gradually learn how to enjoy sex – on their own terms...

Featuring corporal punishment, bondage, defloration, urination and non-consensual sex, *Academy of Lust* suits a sophisticated erotic taste and is a superb BDSM read.

Orderline: 0800 026 25 24
Email: eps@leadline.co.uk
Post: EPS, 54 New Street,
Worcester WR1 2DL

Call and ask about our great Past Venus Multiple Buy Deals! All Past Venus Press paperbacks are priced at £7.50 plus p&p, but our friendly staff are available to advise you about the best savings you can make with a multiple purchase, as a Gold Club member – or both!

Call 0800 026 25 24 (UK only) to find out more or visit our website at

www.eroticprints.org